The Story of
SHERLOCK HOLMES
The Famous Detective

Sherlock Holmes and his helpful friend Dr. John Watson are fictional characters created by British writer Sir Arthur Conan Doyle. Doyle published his first novel about the pair, *A Study in Scarlet*, in 1887, and it became very successful. Doyle went on to write fifty-six short stories, as well as three more novels about Holmes's adventures—*The Sign of Four* (1890), *The Hound of the Baskervilles* (1902), and *The Valley of Fear* (1915).

Sherlock Holmes and Dr. Watson have become some of the most famous book characters of all time. Holmes spent most of his time solving mysteries, but he also had a wide array of hobbies, such as playing the violin, boxing, and sword fighting. Watson, a retired army doctor, met Holmes through a mutual friend when Holmes was looking for a roommate. Watson lived with Holmes for several years at 221B Baker Street before marrying and moving out. However, after his marriage, Watson continued to assist Holmes with his cases.

The original versions of the Sherlock Holmes stories are still printed, and many have been made into movies and television shows. Readers continue to be impressed by Holmes's detective methods of observation and scientific reason.

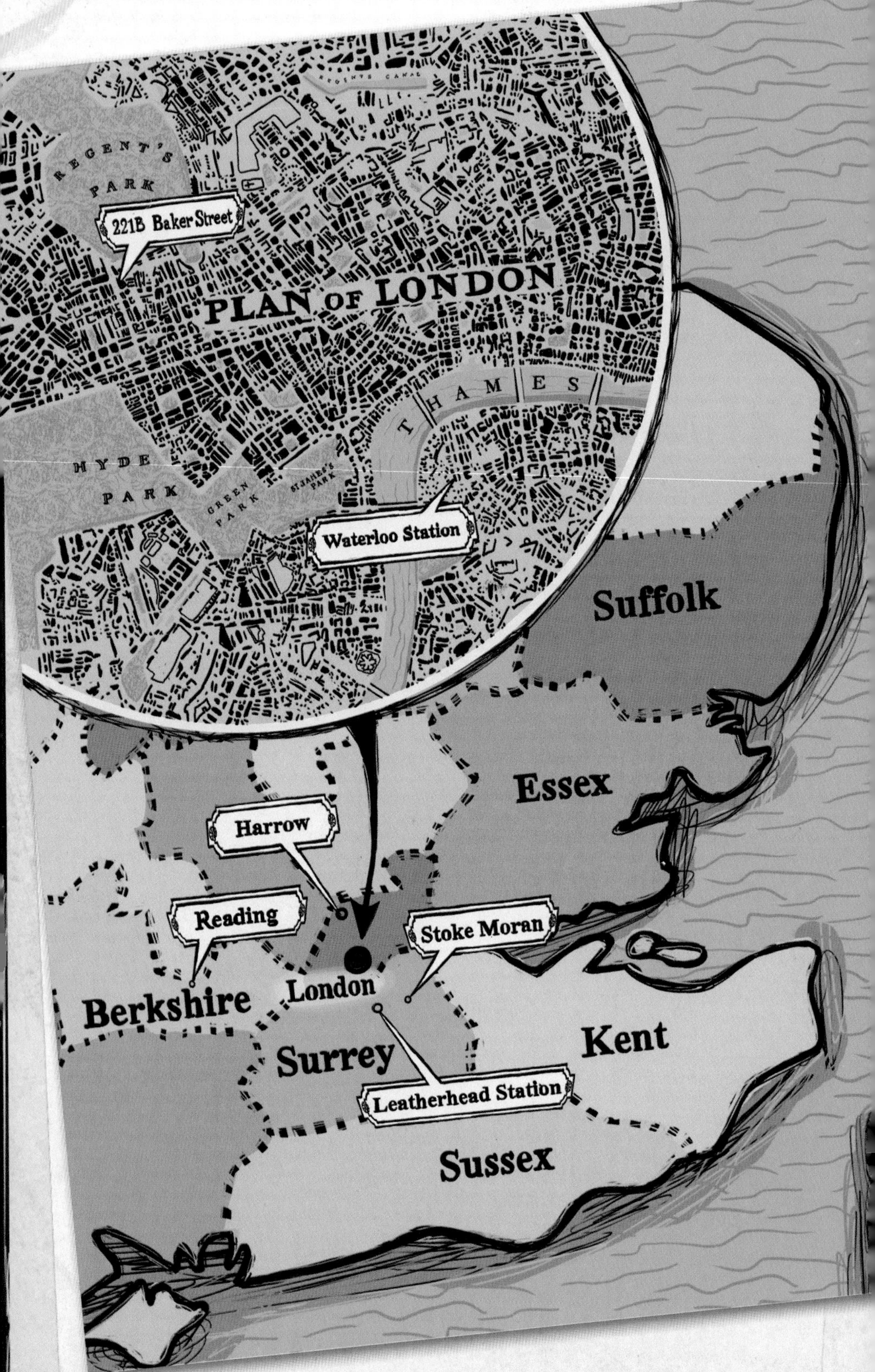
PLAN OF LONDON
REGENT'S PARK
REGENTS CANAL
221B Baker Street
HYDE PARK
GREEN PARK
ST JAMES'S PARK
THAMES
Waterloo Station
Suffolk
Essex
Harrow
Reading
Stoke Moran
London
Berkshire
Kent
Surrey
Leatherhead Station
Sussex

CHARACTER LIST

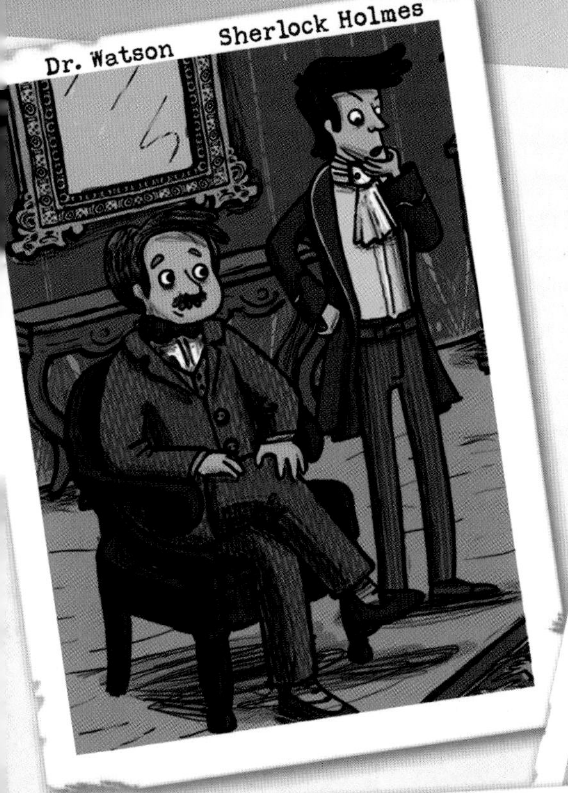
Dr. Watson
Sherlock Holmes

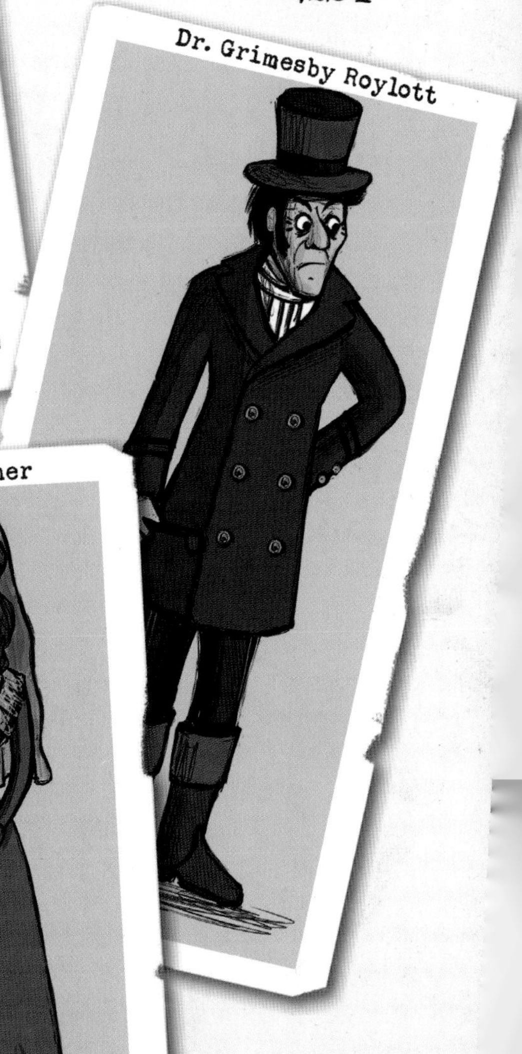
Dr. Grimesby Roylott

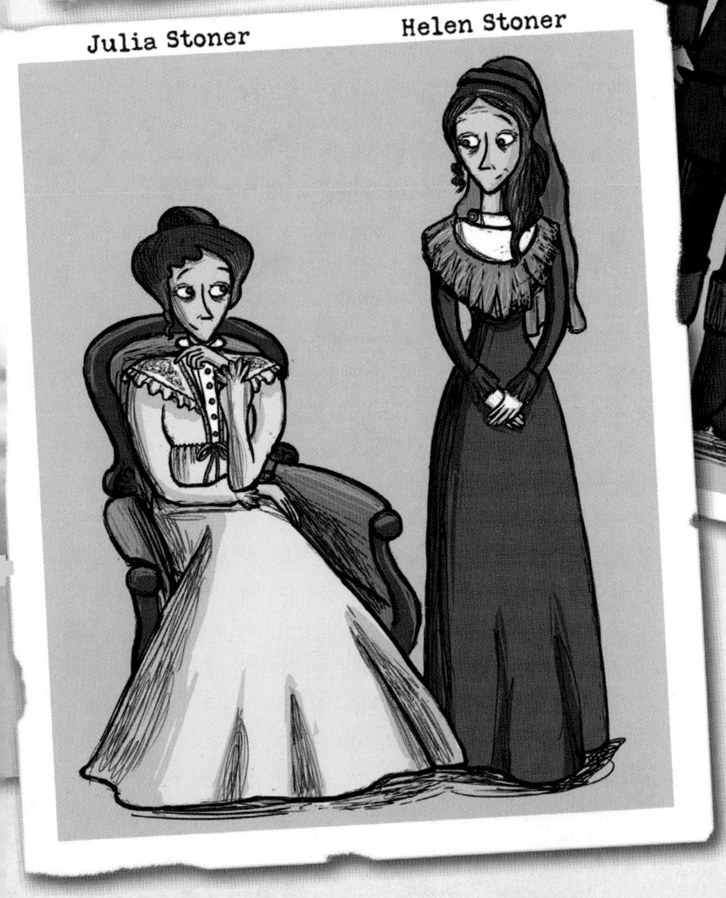
Julia Stoner
Helen Stoner

From the Desk of
John H. Watson, M.D.

My name is Dr. John H. Watson. For several years, I have been assisting my friend, Sherlock Holmes, in solving mysteries throughout the bustling city of London and beyond. Holmes is a peculiar man—always questioning and reasoning his way through various problems. But when I first met him in 1878, I was immediately intrigued by his oddities.

Holmes has always been more daring than I, and his logical deduction never ceases to amaze me. I have begun writing down all of the adventures I have with Holmes. This is one of those stories.

Sincerely,

Dr. Watson

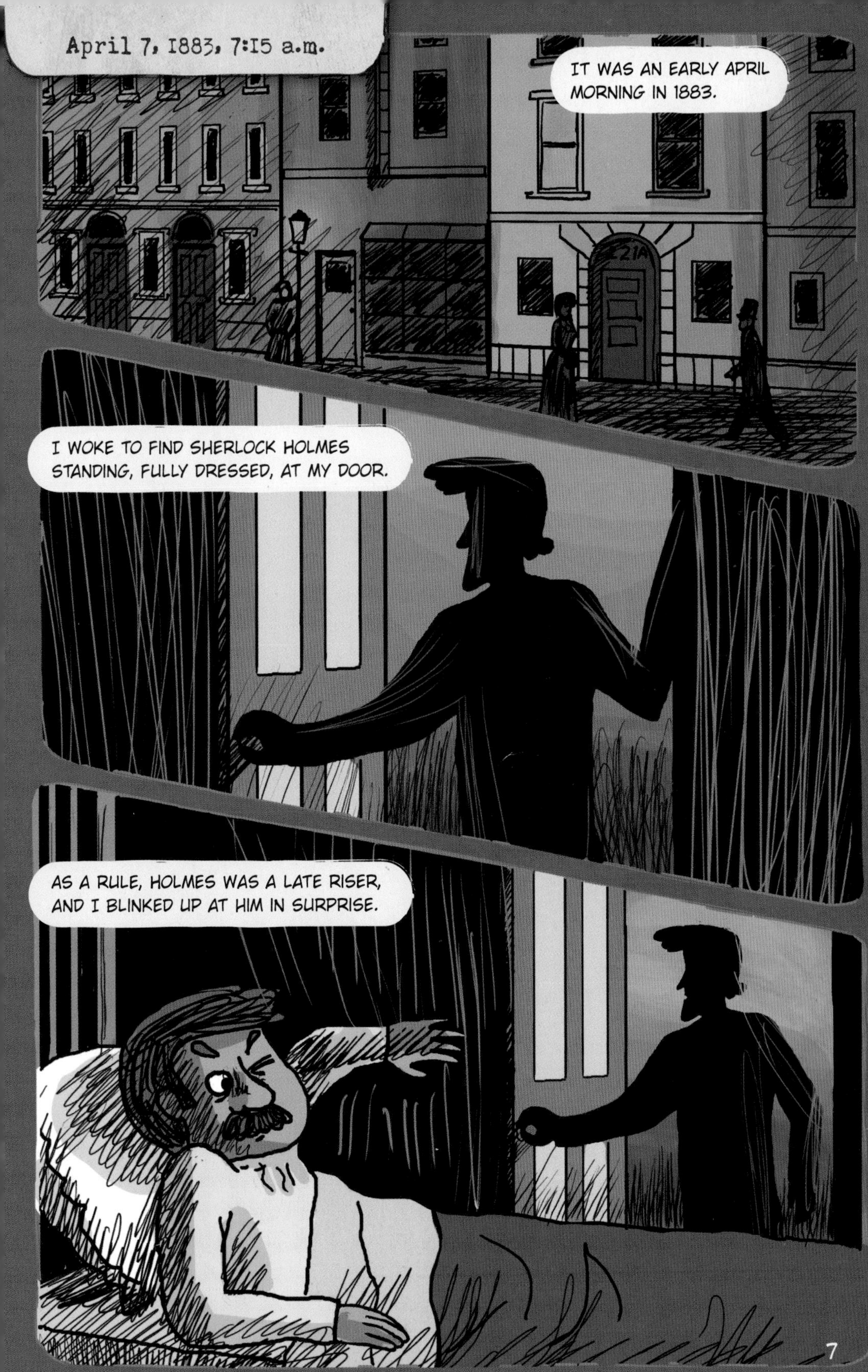
April 7, 1883, 7:15 a.m.
IT WAS AN EARLY APRIL MORNING IN 1883.
221A
I WOKE TO FIND SHERLOCK HOLMES STANDING, FULLY DRESSED, AT MY DOOR.
AS A RULE, HOLMES WAS A LATE RISER, AND I BLINKED UP AT HIM IN SURPRISE.

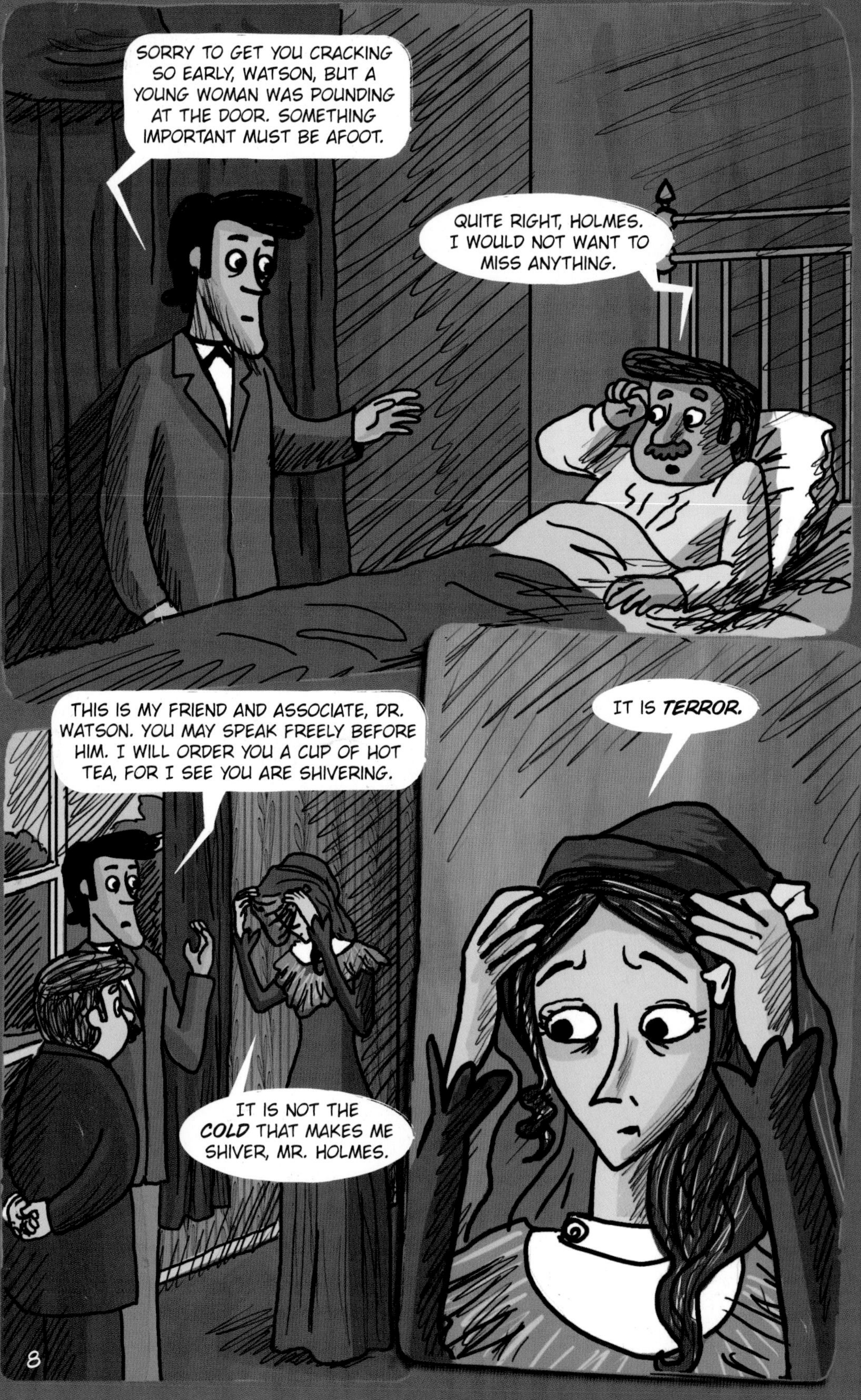
SORRY TO GET YOU CRACKING SO EARLY, WATSON, BUT A YOUNG WOMAN WAS POUNDING AT THE DOOR. SOMETHING IMPORTANT MUST BE AFOOT.
QUITE RIGHT, HOLMES. I WOULD NOT WANT TO MISS ANYTHING.
THIS IS MY FRIEND AND ASSOCIATE, DR. WATSON. YOU MAY SPEAK FREELY BEFORE HIM. I WILL ORDER YOU A CUP OF HOT TEA, FOR I SEE YOU ARE SHIVERING.
IT IS NOT THE *COLD* THAT MAKES ME SHIVER, MR. HOLMES.
IT IS ***TERROR.***

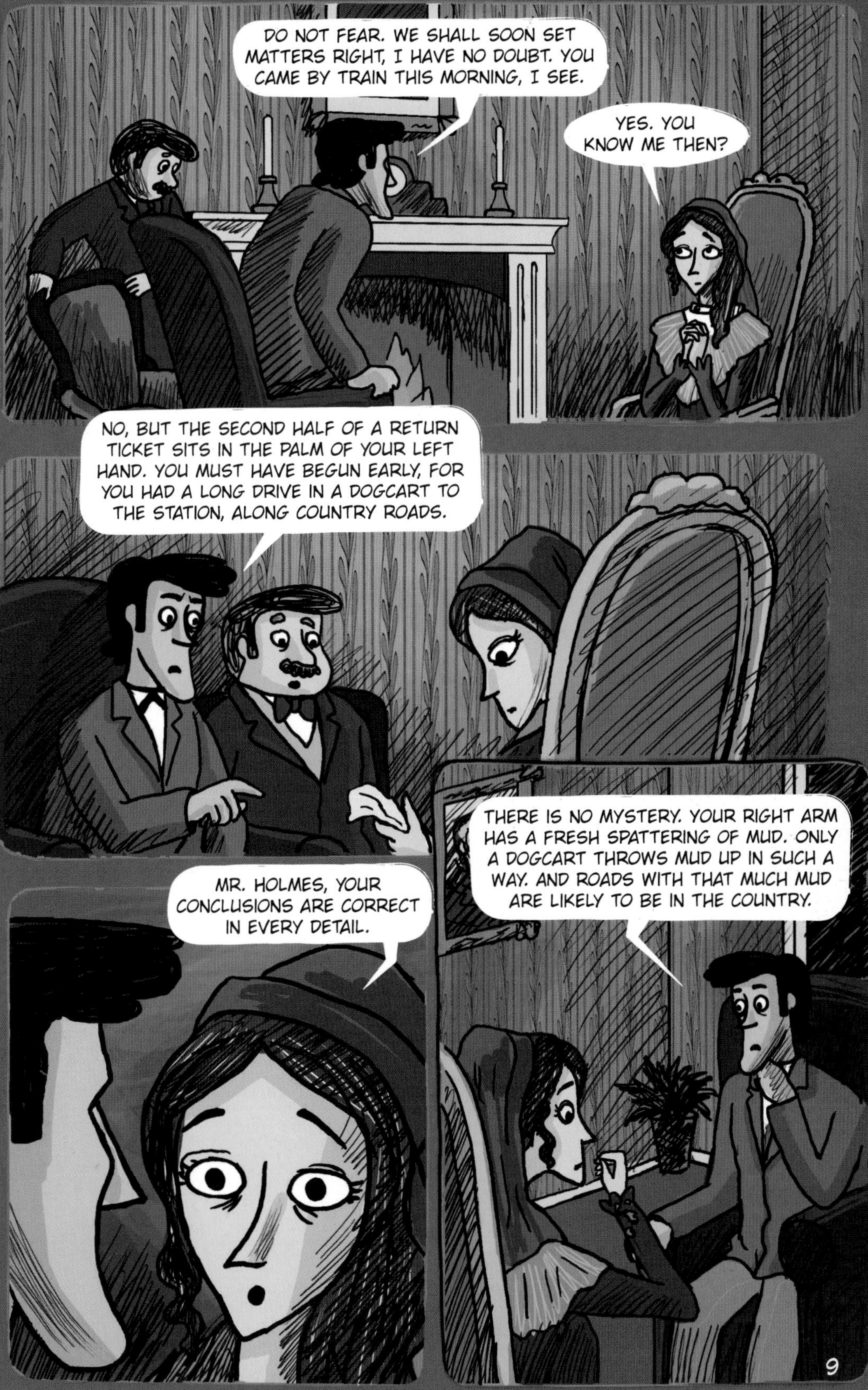

DO NOT FEAR. WE SHALL SOON SET MATTERS RIGHT, I HAVE NO DOUBT. YOU CAME BY TRAIN THIS MORNING, I SEE.
YES. YOU KNOW ME THEN?
NO, BUT THE SECOND HALF OF A RETURN TICKET SITS IN THE PALM OF YOUR LEFT HAND. YOU MUST HAVE BEGUN EARLY, FOR YOU HAD A LONG DRIVE IN A DOGCART TO THE STATION, ALONG COUNTRY ROADS.
MR. HOLMES, YOUR CONCLUSIONS ARE CORRECT IN EVERY DETAIL.
THERE IS NO MYSTERY. YOUR RIGHT ARM HAS A FRESH SPATTERING OF MUD. ONLY A DOGCART THROWS MUD UP IN SUCH A WAY. AND ROADS WITH THAT MUCH MUD ARE LIKELY TO BE IN THE COUNTRY.

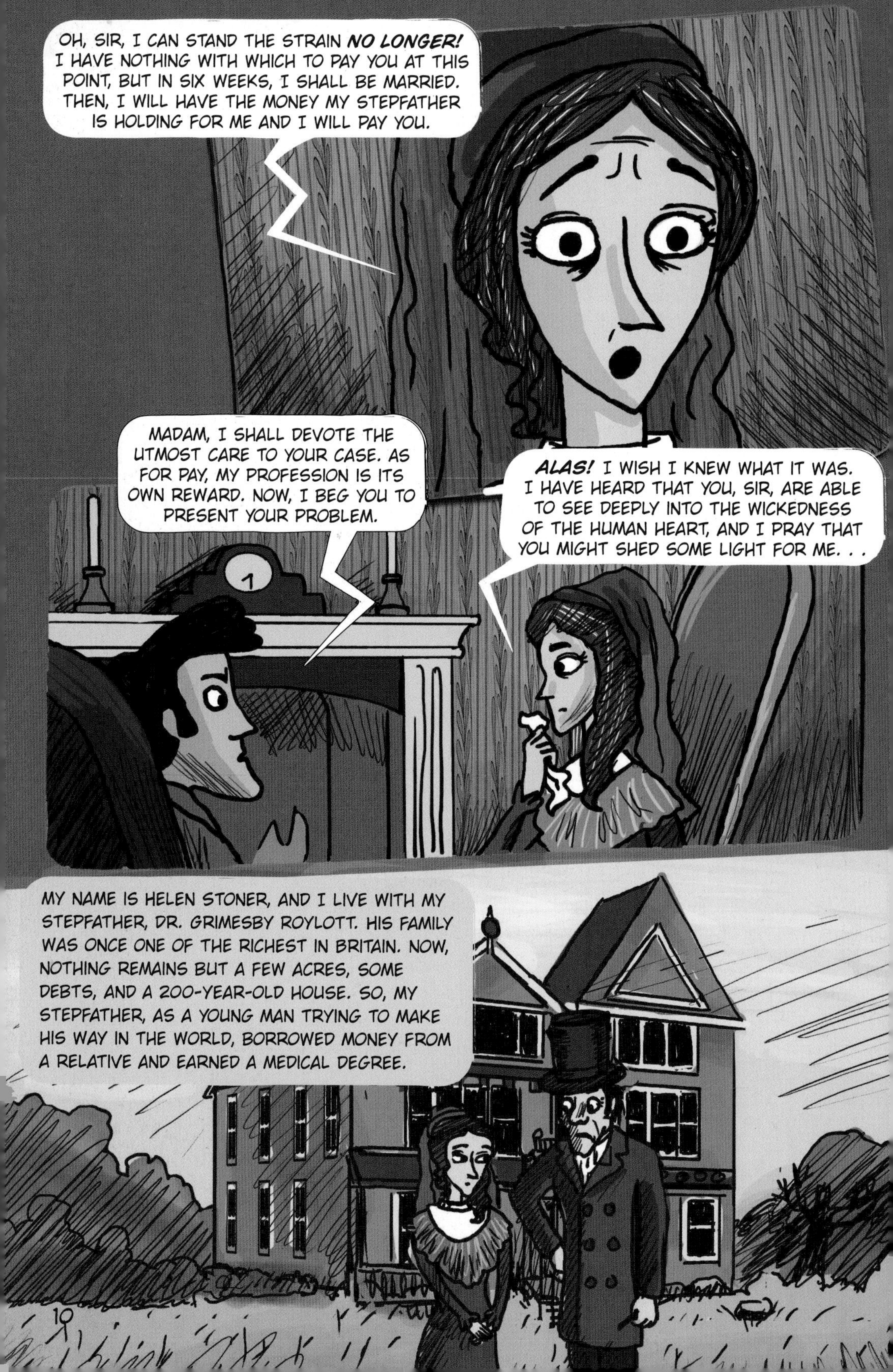

OH, SIR, I CAN STAND THE STRAIN **NO LONGER!** I HAVE NOTHING WITH WHICH TO PAY YOU AT THIS POINT, BUT IN SIX WEEKS, I SHALL BE MARRIED. THEN, I WILL HAVE THE MONEY MY STEPFATHER IS HOLDING FOR ME AND I WILL PAY YOU.
MADAM, I SHALL DEVOTE THE UTMOST CARE TO YOUR CASE. AS FOR PAY, MY PROFESSION IS ITS OWN REWARD. NOW, I BEG YOU TO PRESENT YOUR PROBLEM.
ALAS! I WISH I KNEW WHAT IT WAS. I HAVE HEARD THAT YOU, SIR, ARE ABLE TO SEE DEEPLY INTO THE WICKEDNESS OF THE HUMAN HEART, AND I PRAY THAT YOU MIGHT SHED SOME LIGHT FOR ME. . .
MY NAME IS HELEN STONER, AND I LIVE WITH MY STEPFATHER, DR. GRIMESBY ROYLOTT. HIS FAMILY WAS ONCE ONE OF THE RICHEST IN BRITAIN. NOW, NOTHING REMAINS BUT A FEW ACRES, SOME DEBTS, AND A 200-YEAR-OLD HOUSE. SO, MY STEPFATHER, AS A YOUNG MAN TRYING TO MAKE HIS WAY IN THE WORLD, BORROWED MONEY FROM A RELATIVE AND EARNED A MEDICAL DEGREE.

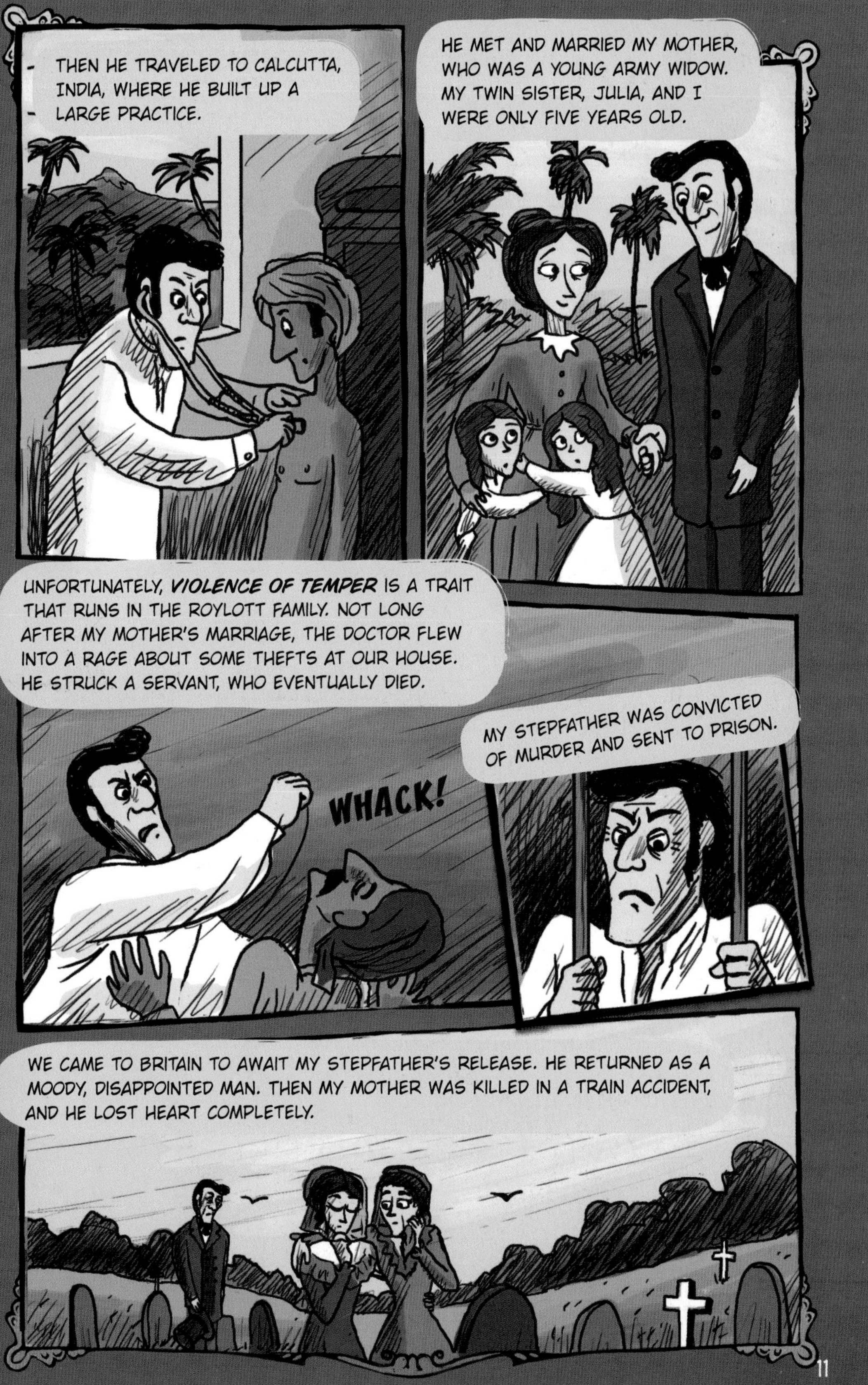
THEN HE TRAVELED TO CALCUTTA, INDIA, WHERE HE BUILT UP A LARGE PRACTICE.
HE MET AND MARRIED MY MOTHER, WHO WAS A YOUNG ARMY WIDOW. MY TWIN SISTER, JULIA, AND I WERE ONLY FIVE YEARS OLD.
UNFORTUNATELY, ***VIOLENCE OF TEMPER*** IS A TRAIT THAT RUNS IN THE ROYLOTT FAMILY. NOT LONG AFTER MY MOTHER'S MARRIAGE, THE DOCTOR FLEW INTO A RAGE ABOUT SOME THEFTS AT OUR HOUSE. HE STRUCK A SERVANT, WHO EVENTUALLY DIED.
WHACK!
MY STEPFATHER WAS CONVICTED OF MURDER AND SENT TO PRISON.
WE CAME TO BRITAIN TO AWAIT MY STEPFATHER'S RELEASE. HE RETURNED AS A MOODY, DISAPPOINTED MAN. THEN MY MOTHER WAS KILLED IN A TRAIN ACCIDENT, AND HE LOST HEART COMPLETELY.

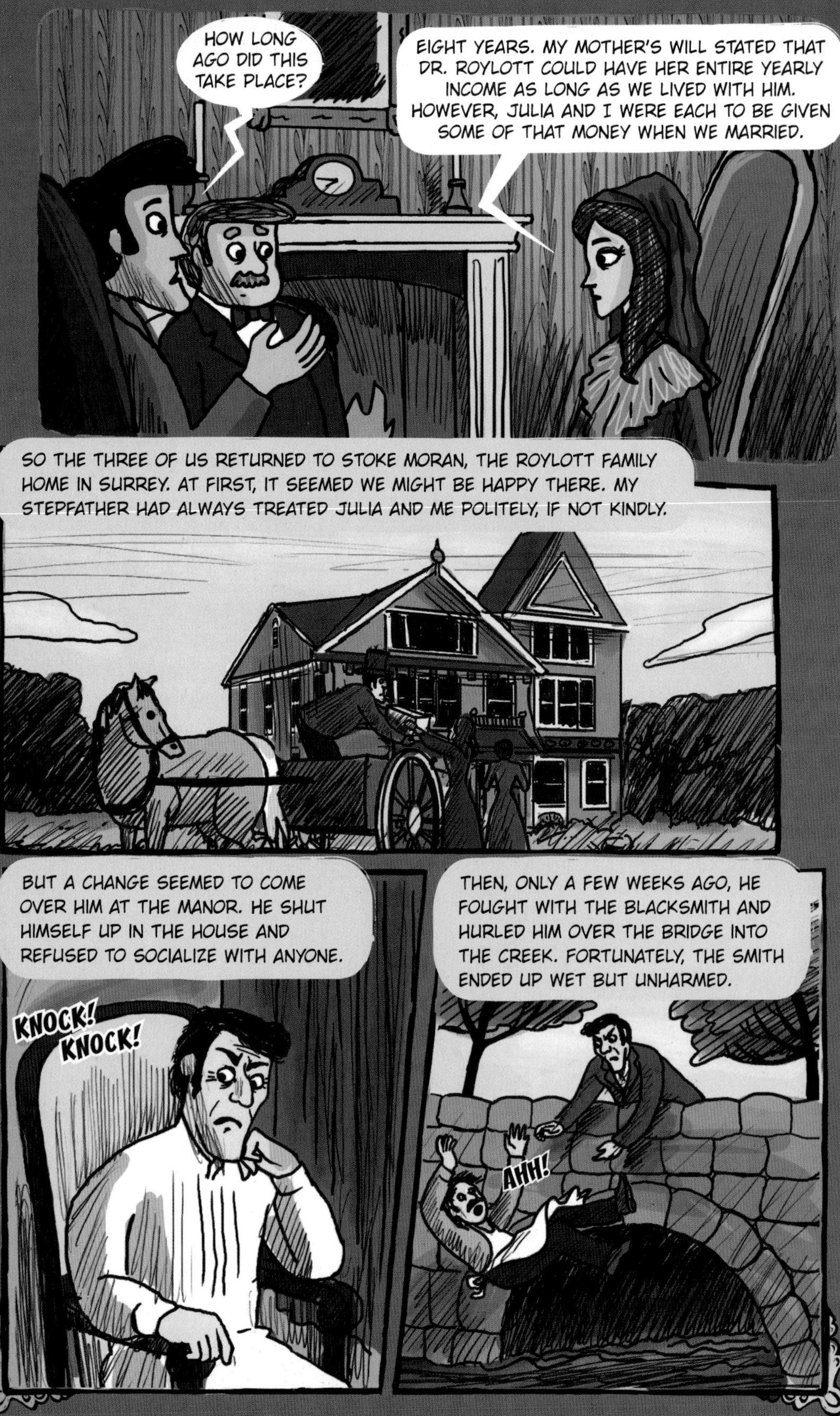
HOW LONG AGO DID THIS TAKE PLACE?
EIGHT YEARS. MY MOTHER'S WILL STATED THAT DR. ROYLOTT COULD HAVE HER ENTIRE YEARLY INCOME AS LONG AS WE LIVED WITH HIM. HOWEVER, JULIA AND I WERE EACH TO BE GIVEN SOME OF THAT MONEY WHEN WE MARRIED.
SO THE THREE OF US RETURNED TO STOKE MORAN, THE ROYLOTT FAMILY HOME IN SURREY. AT FIRST, IT SEEMED WE MIGHT BE HAPPY THERE. MY STEPFATHER HAD ALWAYS TREATED JULIA AND ME POLITELY, IF NOT KINDLY.
BUT A CHANGE SEEMED TO COME OVER HIM AT THE MANOR. HE SHUT HIMSELF UP IN THE HOUSE AND REFUSED TO SOCIALIZE WITH ANYONE.
KNOCK! KNOCK!
THEN, ONLY A FEW WEEKS AGO, HE FOUGHT WITH THE BLACKSMITH AND HURLED HIM OVER THE BRIDGE INTO THE CREEK. FORTUNATELY, THE SMITH ENDED UP WET BUT UNHARMED.
AHH!

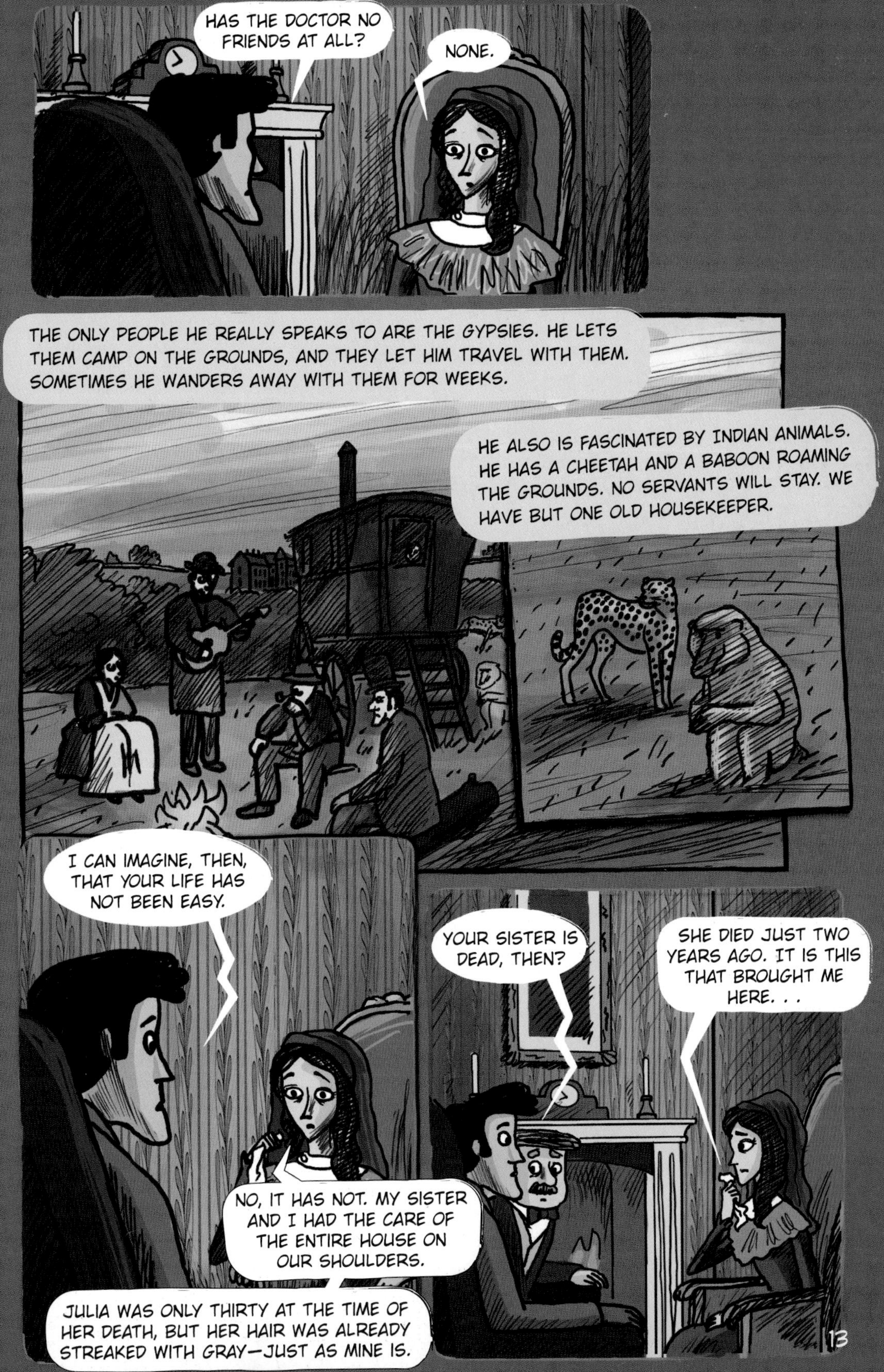
HAS THE DOCTOR NO FRIENDS AT ALL?
NONE.
THE ONLY PEOPLE HE REALLY SPEAKS TO ARE THE GYPSIES. HE LETS THEM CAMP ON THE GROUNDS, AND THEY LET HIM TRAVEL WITH THEM. SOMETIMES HE WANDERS AWAY WITH THEM FOR WEEKS.
HE ALSO IS FASCINATED BY INDIAN ANIMALS. HE HAS A CHEETAH AND A BABOON ROAMING THE GROUNDS. NO SERVANTS WILL STAY. WE HAVE BUT ONE OLD HOUSEKEEPER.
I CAN IMAGINE, THEN, THAT YOUR LIFE HAS NOT BEEN EASY.
NO, IT HAS NOT. MY SISTER AND I HAD THE CARE OF THE ENTIRE HOUSE ON OUR SHOULDERS.
JULIA WAS ONLY THIRTY AT THE TIME OF HER DEATH, BUT HER HAIR WAS ALREADY STREAKED WITH GRAY—JUST AS MINE IS.
YOUR SISTER IS DEAD, THEN?
SHE DIED JUST TWO YEARS AGO. IT IS THIS THAT BROUGHT ME HERE. . .

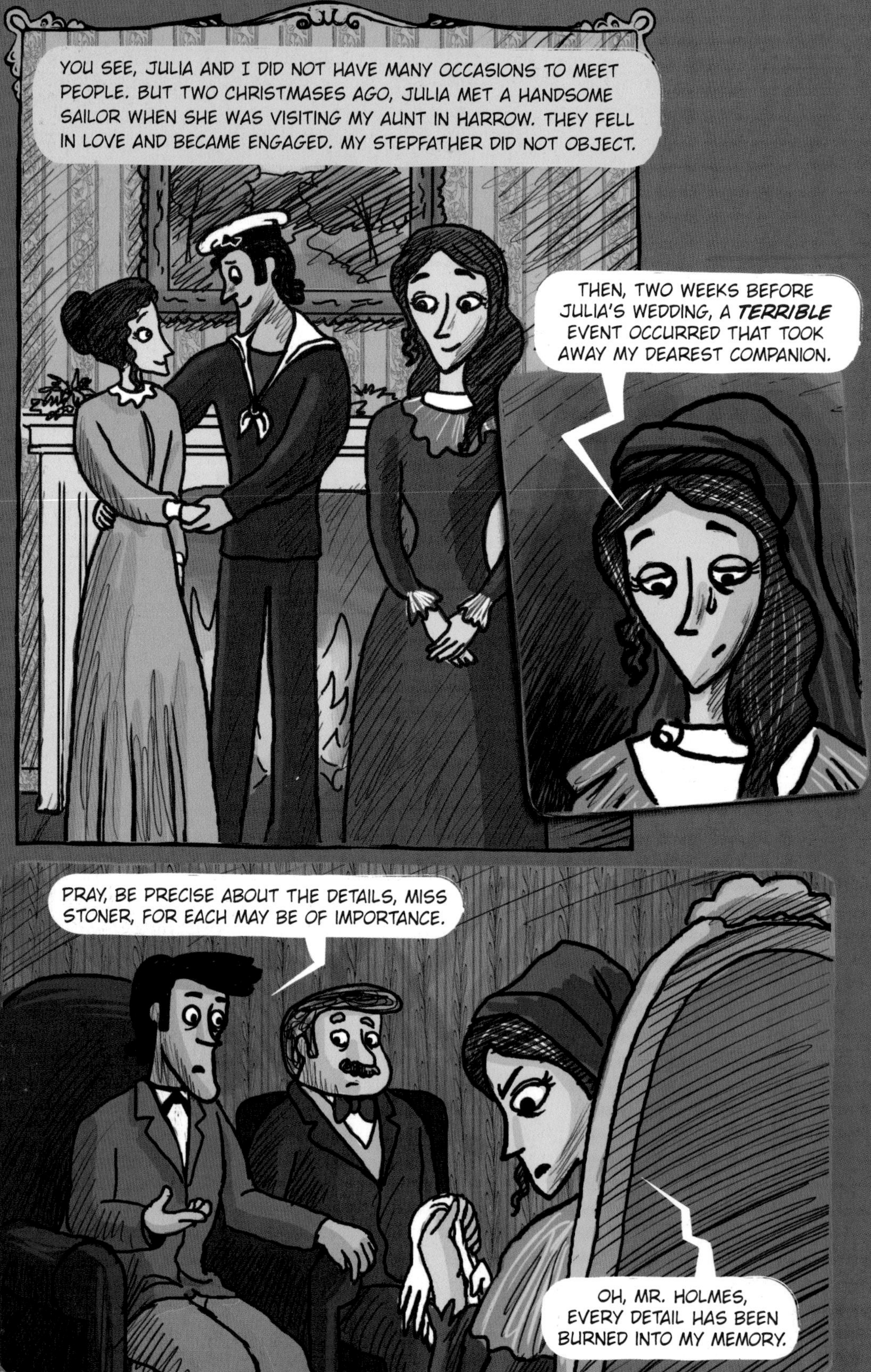
YOU SEE, JULIA AND I DID NOT HAVE MANY OCCASIONS TO MEET PEOPLE. BUT TWO CHRISTMASES AGO, JULIA MET A HANDSOME SAILOR WHEN SHE WAS VISITING MY AUNT IN HARROW. THEY FELL IN LOVE AND BECAME ENGAGED. MY STEPFATHER DID NOT OBJECT.
THEN, TWO WEEKS BEFORE JULIA'S WEDDING, A ***TERRIBLE*** EVENT OCCURRED THAT TOOK AWAY MY DEAREST COMPANION.
PRAY, BE PRECISE ABOUT THE DETAILS, MISS STONER, FOR EACH MAY BE OF IMPORTANCE.
OH, MR. HOLMES, EVERY DETAIL HAS BEEN BURNED INTO MY MEMORY.

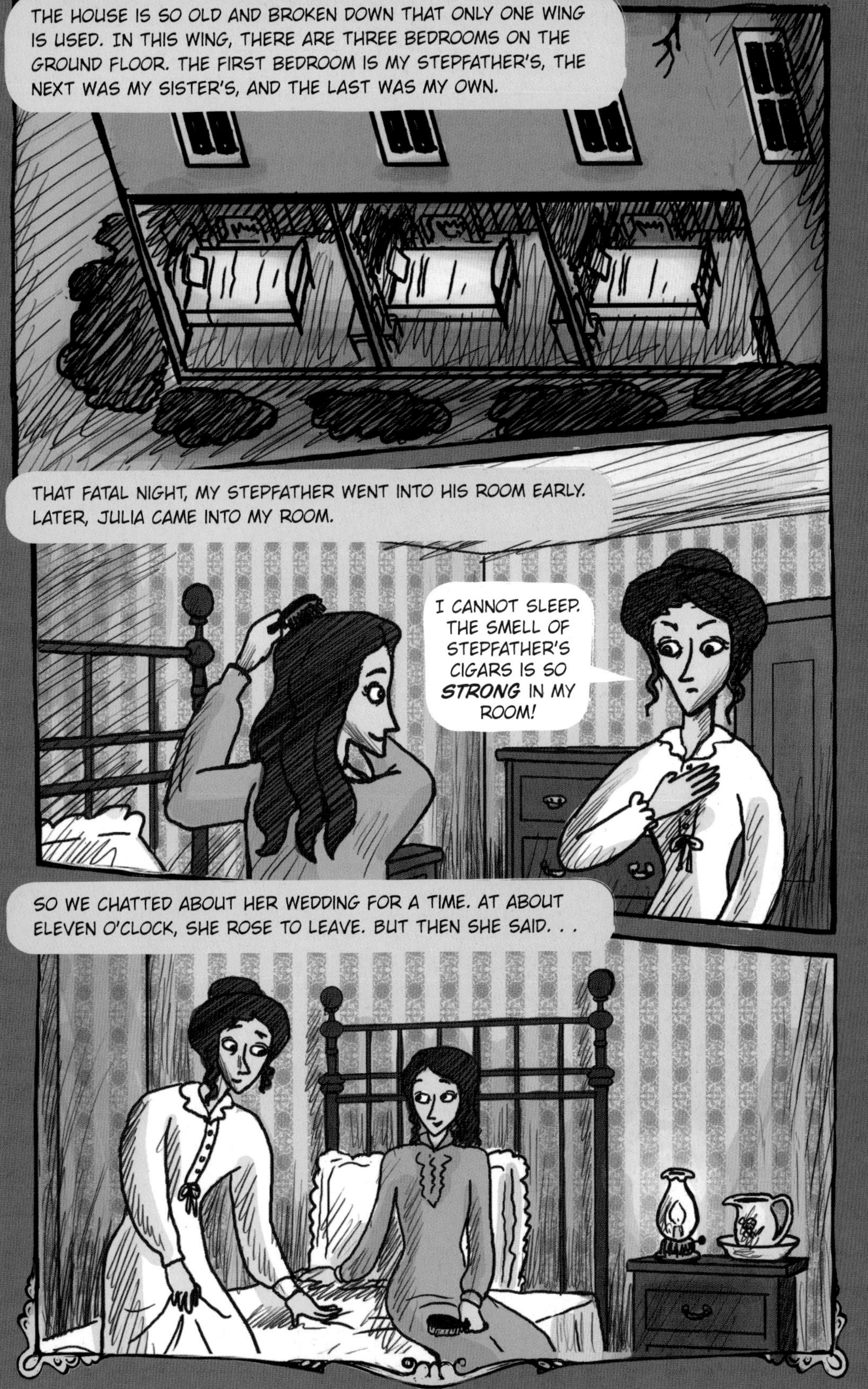
THE HOUSE IS SO OLD AND BROKEN DOWN THAT ONLY ONE WING IS USED. IN THIS WING, THERE ARE THREE BEDROOMS ON THE GROUND FLOOR. THE FIRST BEDROOM IS MY STEPFATHER'S, THE NEXT WAS MY SISTER'S, AND THE LAST WAS MY OWN.
THAT FATAL NIGHT, MY STEPFATHER WENT INTO HIS ROOM EARLY. LATER, JULIA CAME INTO MY ROOM.
I CANNOT SLEEP. THE SMELL OF STEPFATHER'S CIGARS IS SO STRONG IN MY ROOM!
SO WE CHATTED ABOUT HER WEDDING FOR A TIME. AT ABOUT ELEVEN O'CLOCK, SHE ROSE TO LEAVE. BUT THEN SHE SAID. . .

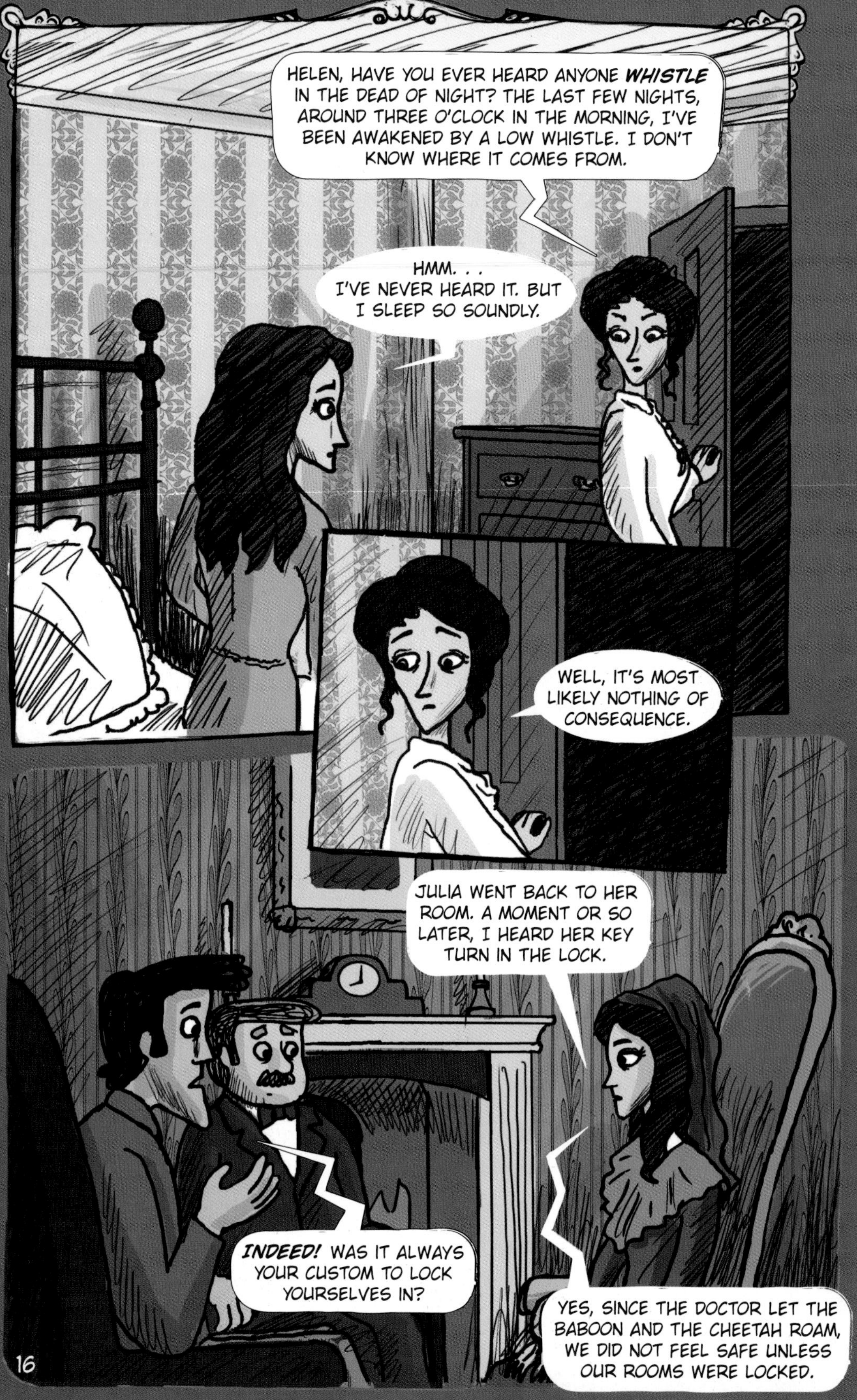
HELEN, HAVE YOU EVER HEARD ANYONE *WHISTLE* IN THE DEAD OF NIGHT? THE LAST FEW NIGHTS, AROUND THREE O'CLOCK IN THE MORNING, I'VE BEEN AWAKENED BY A LOW WHISTLE. I DON'T KNOW WHERE IT COMES FROM.
HMM. . . I'VE NEVER HEARD IT. BUT I SLEEP SO SOUNDLY.
WELL, IT'S MOST LIKELY NOTHING OF CONSEQUENCE.
JULIA WENT BACK TO HER ROOM. A MOMENT OR SO LATER, I HEARD HER KEY TURN IN THE LOCK.
INDEED! WAS IT ALWAYS YOUR CUSTOM TO LOCK YOURSELVES IN?
YES, SINCE THE DOCTOR LET THE BABOON AND THE CHEETAH ROAM, WE DID NOT FEEL SAFE UNLESS OUR ROOMS WERE LOCKED.

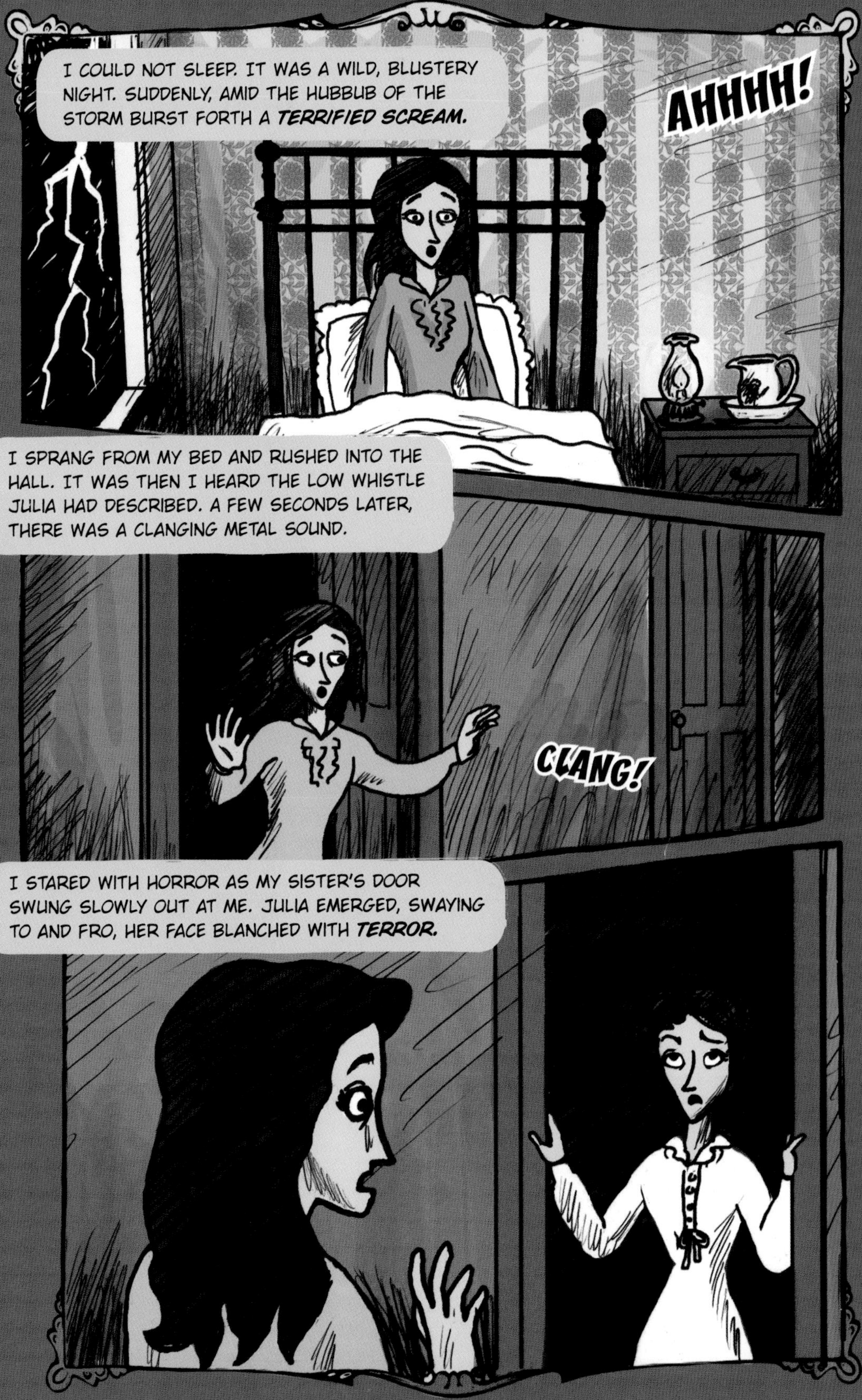
I COULD NOT SLEEP. IT WAS A WILD, BLUSTERY NIGHT. SUDDENLY, AMID THE HUBBUB OF THE STORM BURST FORTH A *TERRIFIED SCREAM.*
AHHHH!
I SPRANG FROM MY BED AND RUSHED INTO THE HALL. IT WAS THEN I HEARD THE LOW WHISTLE JULIA HAD DESCRIBED. A FEW SECONDS LATER, THERE WAS A CLANGING METAL SOUND.
CLANG!
I STARED WITH HORROR AS MY SISTER'S DOOR SWUNG SLOWLY OUT AT ME. JULIA EMERGED, SWAYING TO AND FRO, HER FACE BLANCHED WITH *TERROR.*

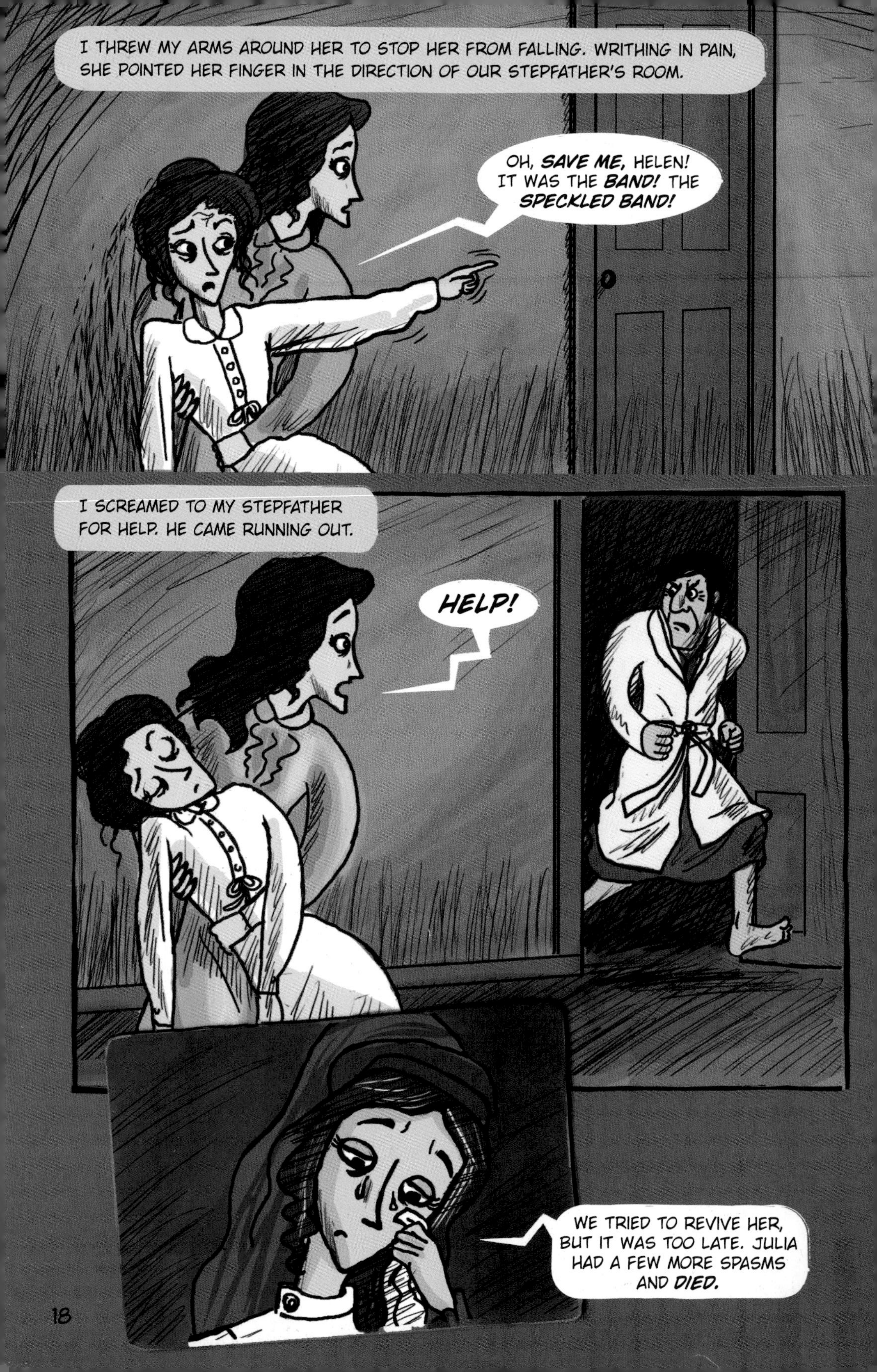
I THREW MY ARMS AROUND HER TO STOP HER FROM FALLING. WRITHING IN PAIN, SHE POINTED HER FINGER IN THE DIRECTION OF OUR STEPFATHER'S ROOM.
OH, SAVE ME, HELEN! IT WAS THE BAND! THE SPECKLED BAND!
I SCREAMED TO MY STEPFATHER FOR HELP. HE CAME RUNNING OUT.
HELP!
WE TRIED TO REVIVE HER, BUT IT WAS TOO LATE. JULIA HAD A FEW MORE SPASMS AND DIED.

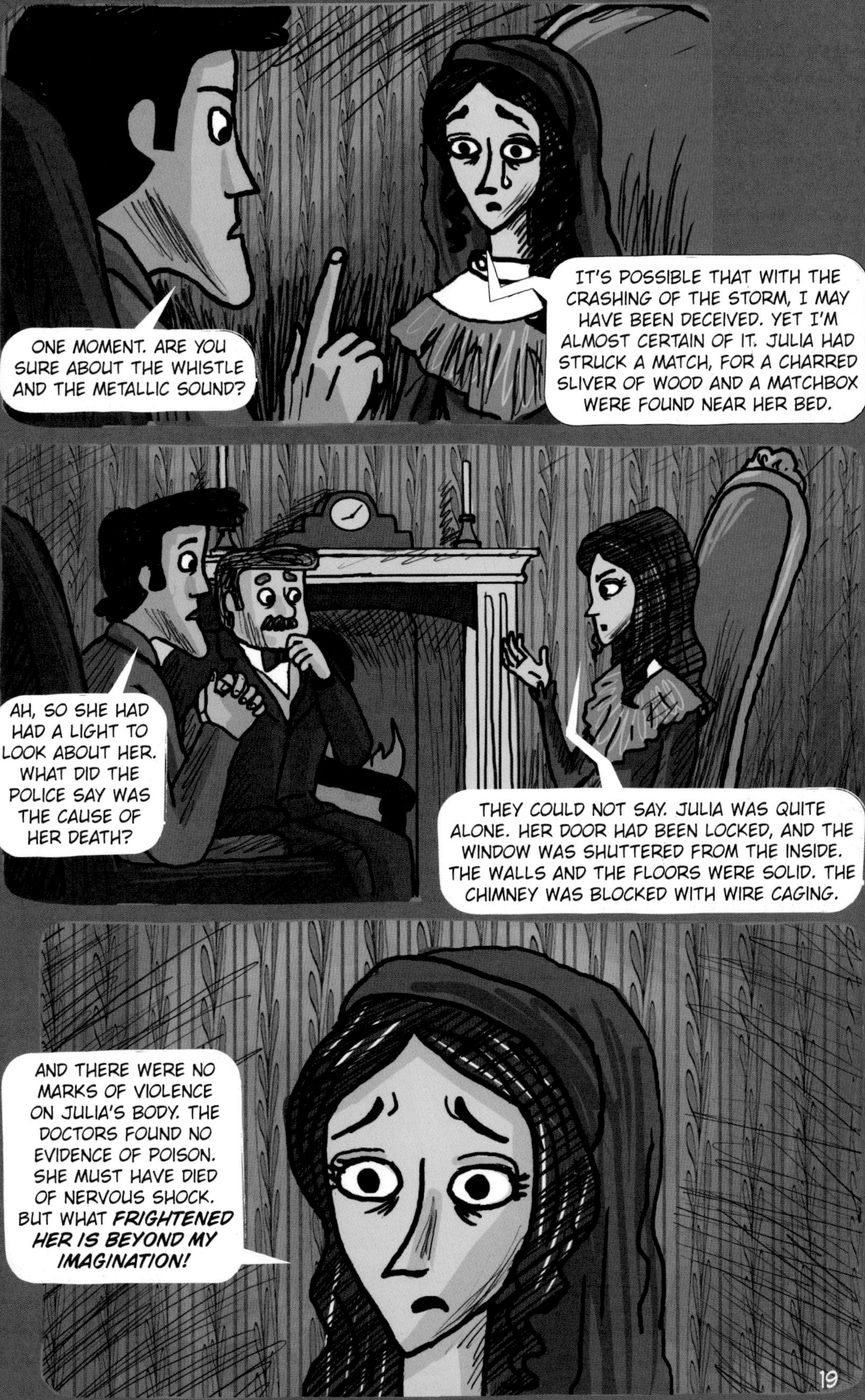
ONE MOMENT. ARE YOU SURE ABOUT THE WHISTLE AND THE METALLIC SOUND?
IT'S POSSIBLE THAT WITH THE CRASHING OF THE STORM, I MAY HAVE BEEN DECEIVED. YET I'M ALMOST CERTAIN OF IT. JULIA HAD STRUCK A MATCH, FOR A CHARRED SLIVER OF WOOD AND A MATCHBOX WERE FOUND NEAR HER BED.
AH, SO SHE HAD HAD A LIGHT TO LOOK ABOUT HER. WHAT DID THE POLICE SAY WAS THE CAUSE OF HER DEATH?
THEY COULD NOT SAY. JULIA WAS QUITE ALONE. HER DOOR HAD BEEN LOCKED, AND THE WINDOW WAS SHUTTERED FROM THE INSIDE. THE WALLS AND THE FLOORS WERE SOLID. THE CHIMNEY WAS BLOCKED WITH WIRE CAGING.
AND THERE WERE NO MARKS OF VIOLENCE ON JULIA'S BODY. THE DOCTORS FOUND NO EVIDENCE OF POISON. SHE MUST HAVE DIED OF NERVOUS SHOCK. BUT WHAT ***FRIGHTENED HER IS BEYOND MY IMAGINATION!***

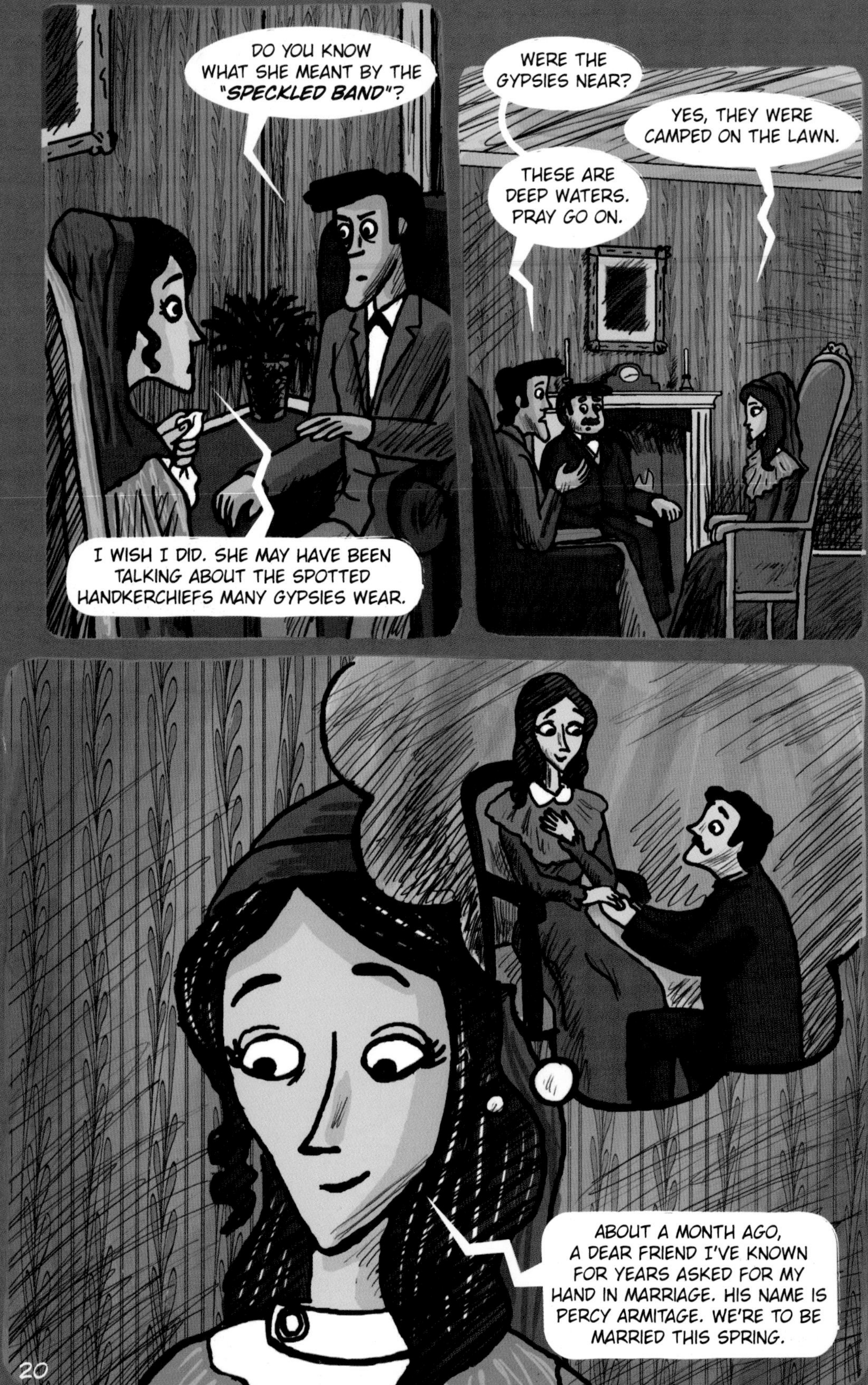
DO YOU KNOW WHAT SHE MEANT BY THE "SPECKLED BAND"?
I WISH I DID. SHE MAY HAVE BEEN TALKING ABOUT THE SPOTTED HANDKERCHIEFS MANY GYPSIES WEAR.
WERE THE GYPSIES NEAR?
YES, THEY WERE CAMPED ON THE LAWN.
THESE ARE DEEP WATERS. PRAY GO ON.
ABOUT A MONTH AGO, A DEAR FRIEND I'VE KNOWN FOR YEARS ASKED FOR MY HAND IN MARRIAGE. HIS NAME IS PERCY ARMITAGE. WE'RE TO BE MARRIED THIS SPRING.

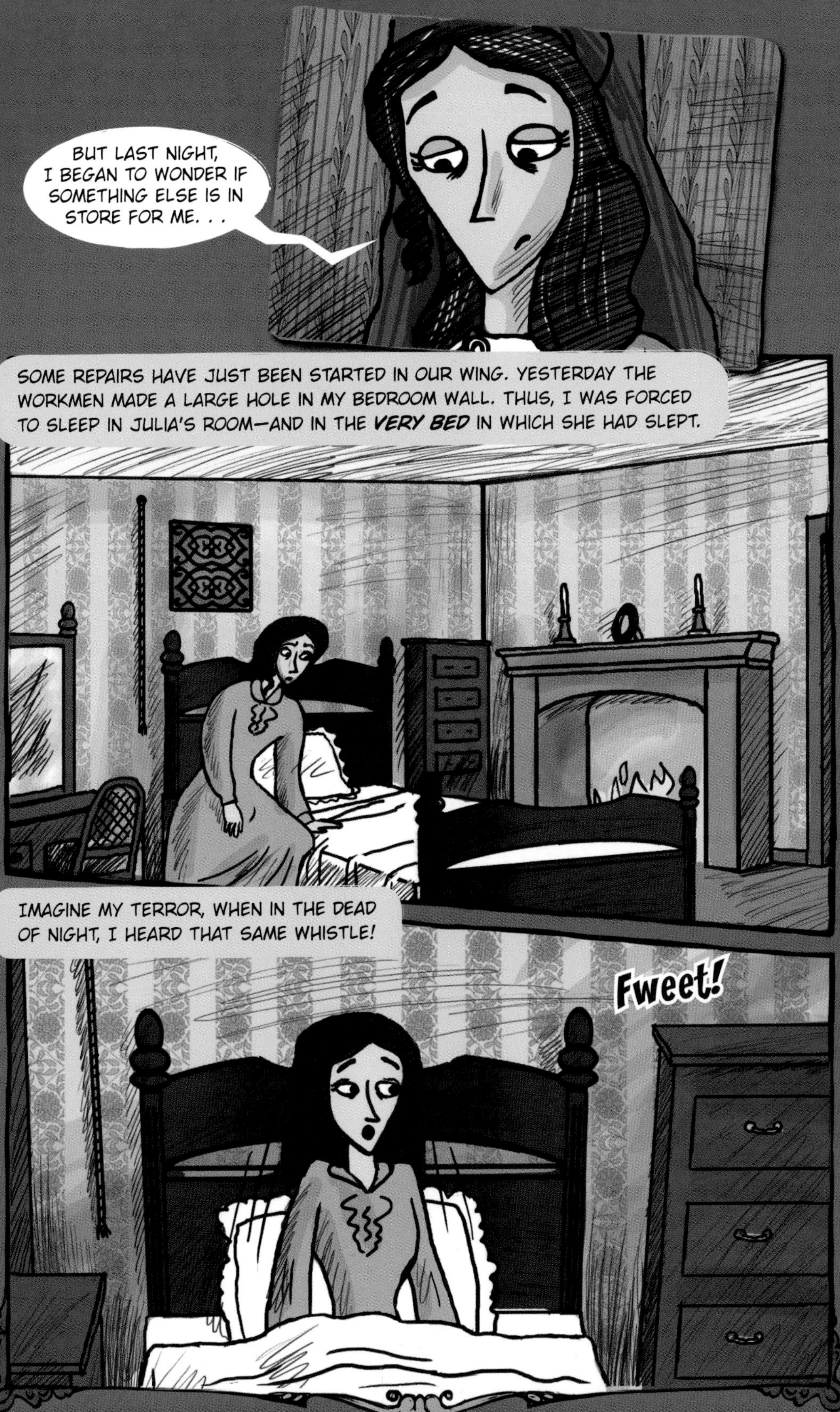
BUT LAST NIGHT, I BEGAN TO WONDER IF SOMETHING ELSE IS IN STORE FOR ME. . .
SOME REPAIRS HAVE JUST BEEN STARTED IN OUR WING. YESTERDAY THE WORKMEN MADE A LARGE HOLE IN MY BEDROOM WALL. THUS, I WAS FORCED TO SLEEP IN JULIA'S ROOM—AND IN THE VERY BED IN WHICH SHE HAD SLEPT.
IMAGINE MY TERROR, WHEN IN THE DEAD OF NIGHT, I HEARD THAT SAME WHISTLE!
Fweet!

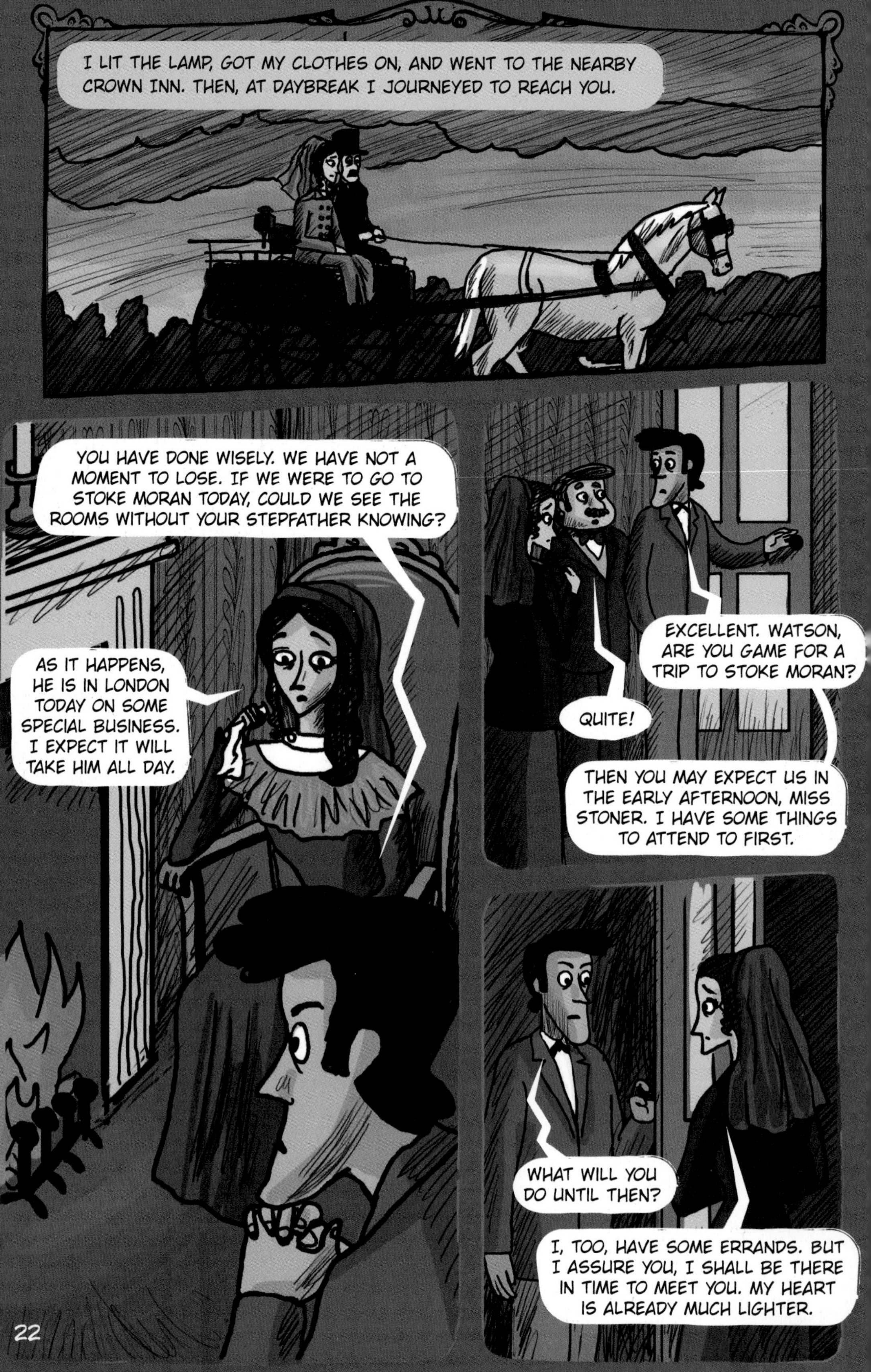

I LIT THE LAMP, GOT MY CLOTHES ON, AND WENT TO THE NEARBY CROWN INN. THEN, AT DAYBREAK I JOURNEYED TO REACH YOU.
YOU HAVE DONE WISELY. WE HAVE NOT A MOMENT TO LOSE. IF WE WERE TO GO TO STOKE MORAN TODAY, COULD WE SEE THE ROOMS WITHOUT YOUR STEPFATHER KNOWING?
AS IT HAPPENS, HE IS IN LONDON TODAY ON SOME SPECIAL BUSINESS. I EXPECT IT WILL TAKE HIM ALL DAY.
EXCELLENT. WATSON, ARE YOU GAME FOR A TRIP TO STOKE MORAN?
QUITE!
THEN YOU MAY EXPECT US IN THE EARLY AFTERNOON, MISS STONER. I HAVE SOME THINGS TO ATTEND TO FIRST.
WHAT WILL YOU DO UNTIL THEN?
I, TOO, HAVE SOME ERRANDS. BUT I ASSURE YOU, I SHALL BE THERE IN TIME TO MEET YOU. MY HEART IS ALREADY MUCH LIGHTER.

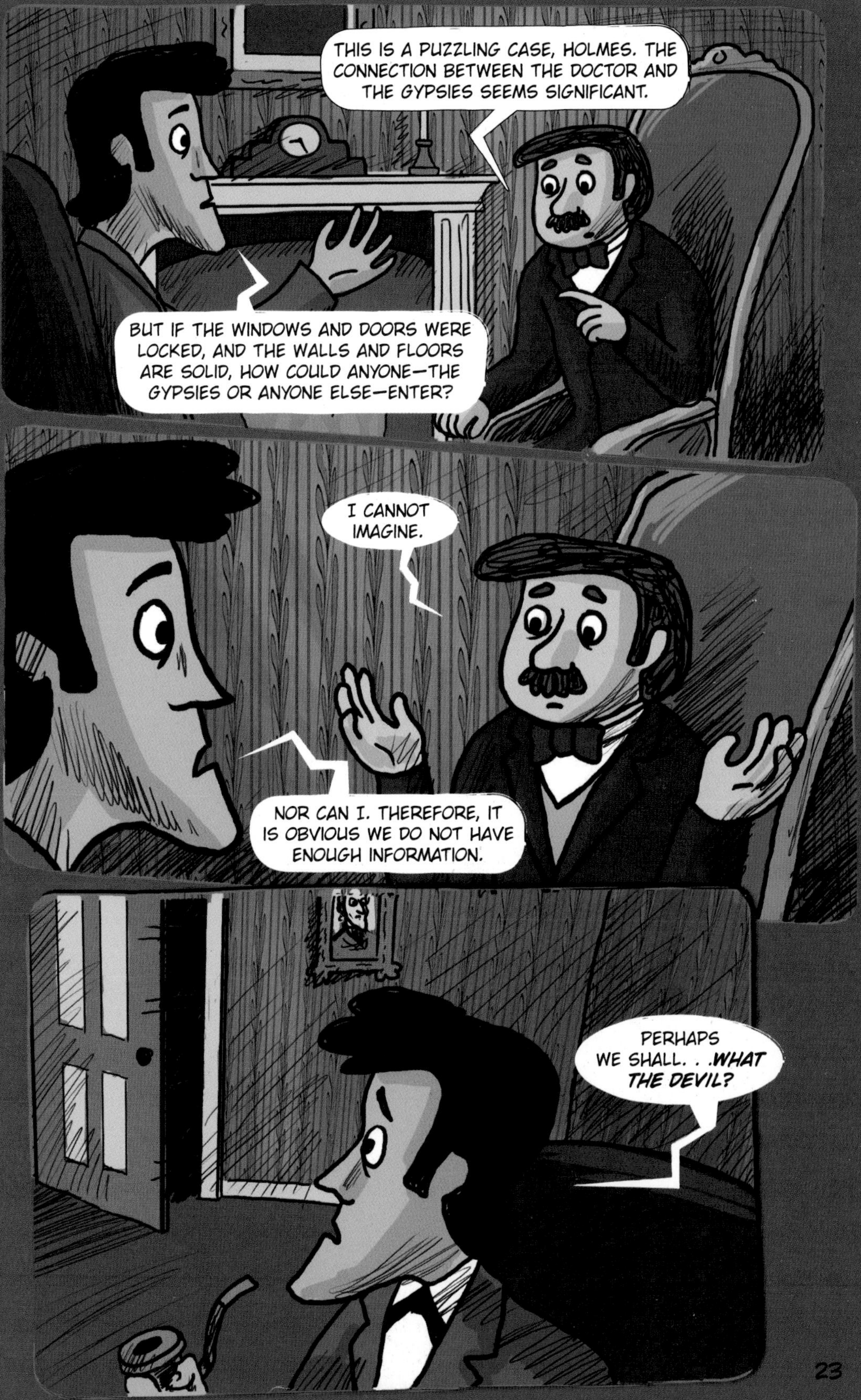
THIS IS A PUZZLING CASE, HOLMES. THE CONNECTION BETWEEN THE DOCTOR AND THE GYPSIES SEEMS SIGNIFICANT.
BUT IF THE WINDOWS AND DOORS WERE LOCKED, AND THE WALLS AND FLOORS ARE SOLID, HOW COULD ANYONE—THE GYPSIES OR ANYONE ELSE—ENTER?
I CANNOT IMAGINE.
NOR CAN I. THEREFORE, IT IS OBVIOUS WE DO NOT HAVE ENOUGH INFORMATION.
PERHAPS WE SHALL. . .*WHAT THE DEVIL?*

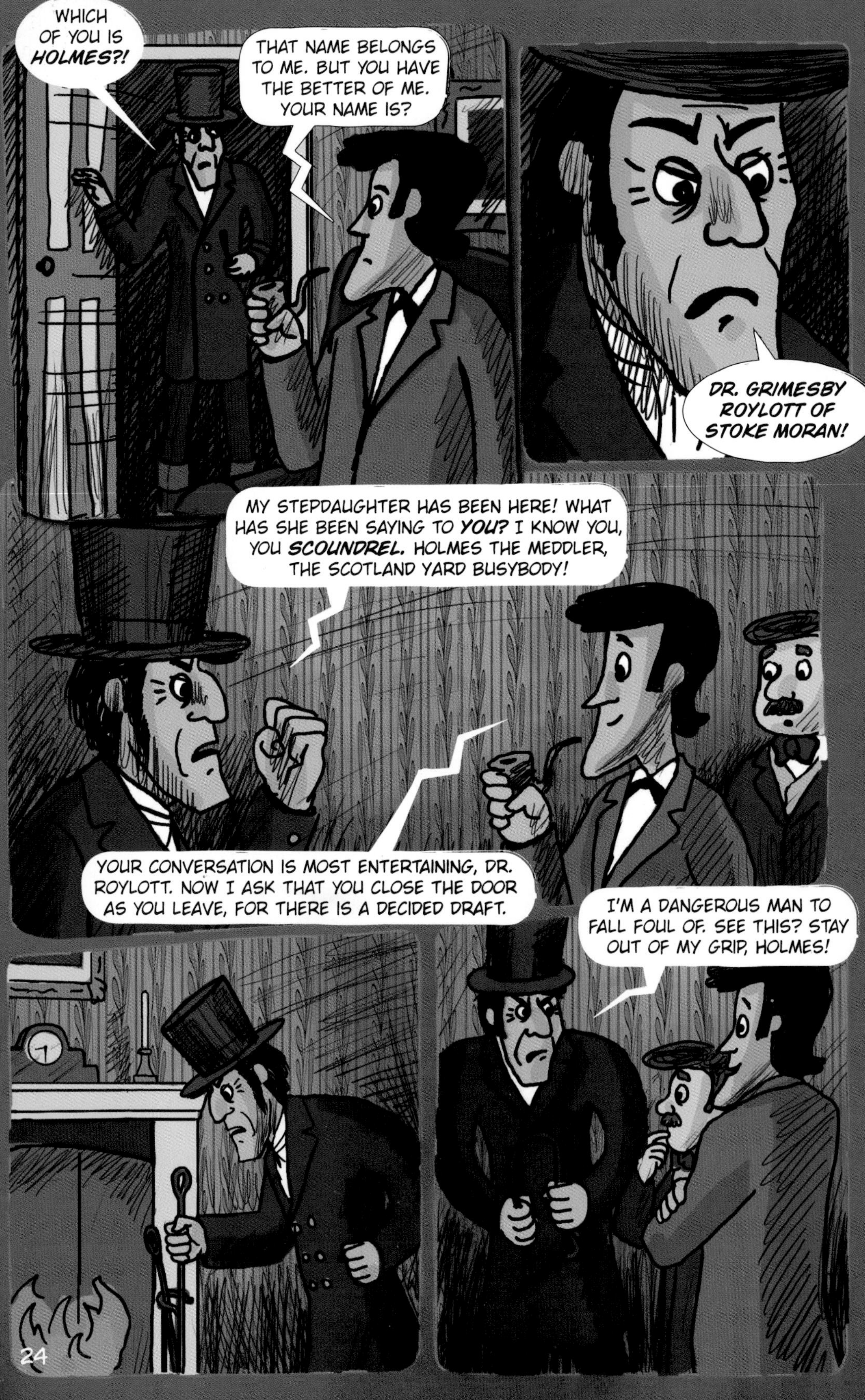
WHICH OF YOU IS **HOLMES?!**
THAT NAME BELONGS TO ME. BUT YOU HAVE THE BETTER OF ME. YOUR NAME IS?
DR. GRIMESBY ROYLOTT OF STOKE MORAN!
MY STEPDAUGHTER HAS BEEN HERE! WHAT HAS SHE BEEN SAYING TO **YOU?** I KNOW YOU, YOU **SCOUNDREL.** HOLMES THE MEDDLER, THE SCOTLAND YARD BUSYBODY!
YOUR CONVERSATION IS MOST ENTERTAINING, DR. ROYLOTT. NOW I ASK THAT YOU CLOSE THE DOOR AS YOU LEAVE, FOR THERE IS A DECIDED DRAFT.
I'M A DANGEROUS MAN TO FALL FOUL OF. SEE THIS? STAY OUT OF MY GRIP, HOLMES!

April 7, 1883, 1:00 p.m.

As abruptly as he had arrived, Roylott
stormed out the door. I must admit I was
a bit shaken by Roylott's demonstration, but
Holmes simply shook his head in amusement. He
strode to the fireplace, picked up the poker,
and with a sudden effort, straightened it. As
long as I've known him, the man continues to
amaze me.

That afternoon Holmes went to see what data
the courts had concerning Julia's death and
Dr. Roylott. He returned at nearly one o'clock
with some useful information. He found the
will of the deceased wife. It stated that each
daughter is to receive 250 pounds sterling per
year after marriage. Originally the estate's
yearly income was 1,000 pounds. However, since
then, the value of the investments had gone
down. They were now worth only 750 pounds per
year.

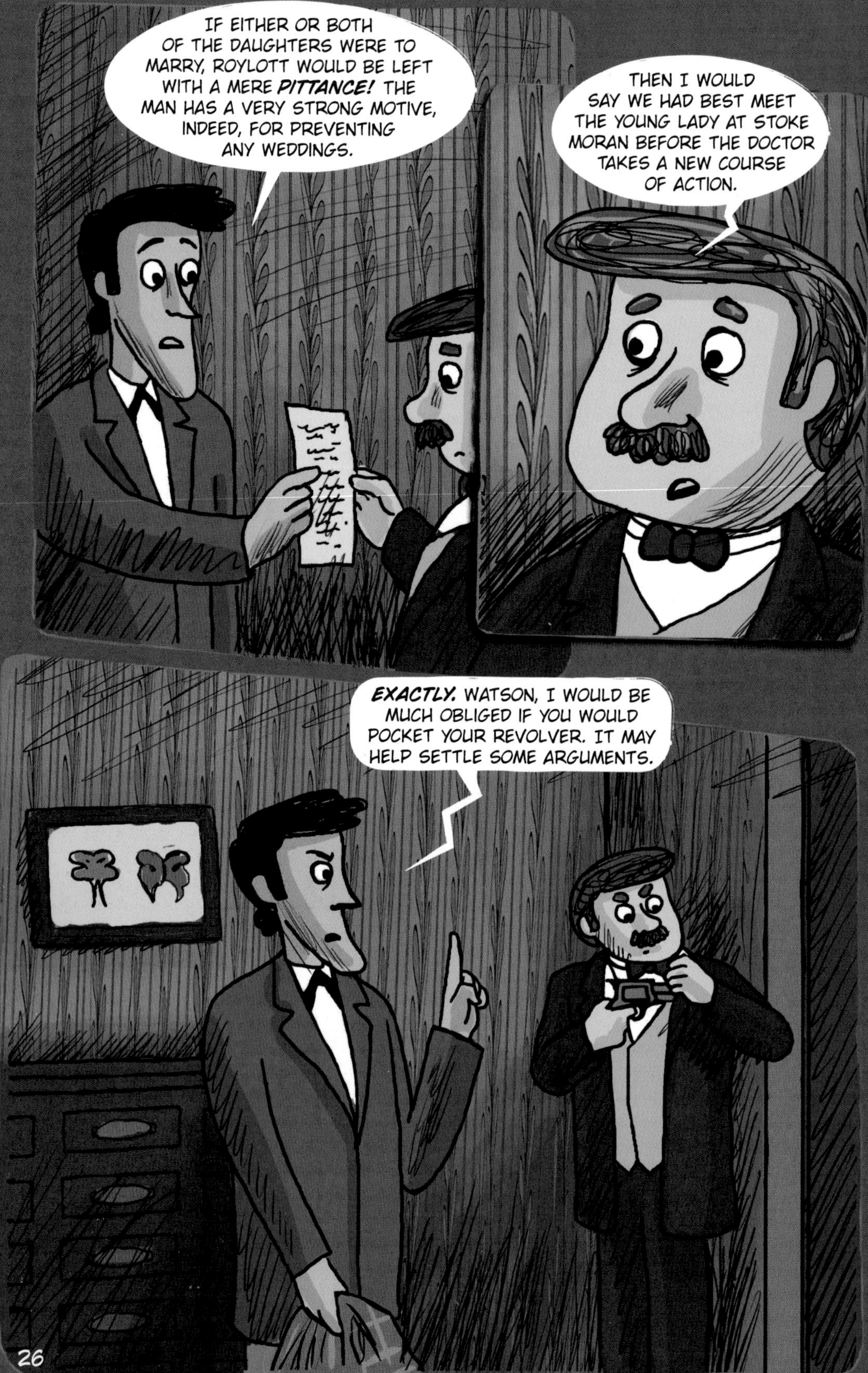
IF EITHER OR BOTH OF THE DAUGHTERS WERE TO MARRY, ROYLOTT WOULD BE LEFT WITH A MERE **PITTANCE!** THE MAN HAS A VERY STRONG MOTIVE, INDEED, FOR PREVENTING ANY WEDDINGS.
THEN I WOULD SAY WE HAD BEST MEET THE YOUNG LADY AT STOKE MORAN BEFORE THE DOCTOR TAKES A NEW COURSE OF ACTION.
EXACTLY. WATSON, I WOULD BE MUCH OBLIGED IF YOU WOULD POCKET YOUR REVOLVER. IT MAY HELP SETTLE SOME ARGUMENTS.

We hailed a cab to Waterloo Station, caught a train for Leatherhead Station, and then hired a carriage to take us to the manor. The perfect spring day seemed a strange contrast to the deathly puzzle of Stoke Moran. What was the low whistle? What had frightened the sister to death? Holmes sat scrunched in his seat the whole way, his hat pulled over his eyes so he could think. I kept quietly to myself.

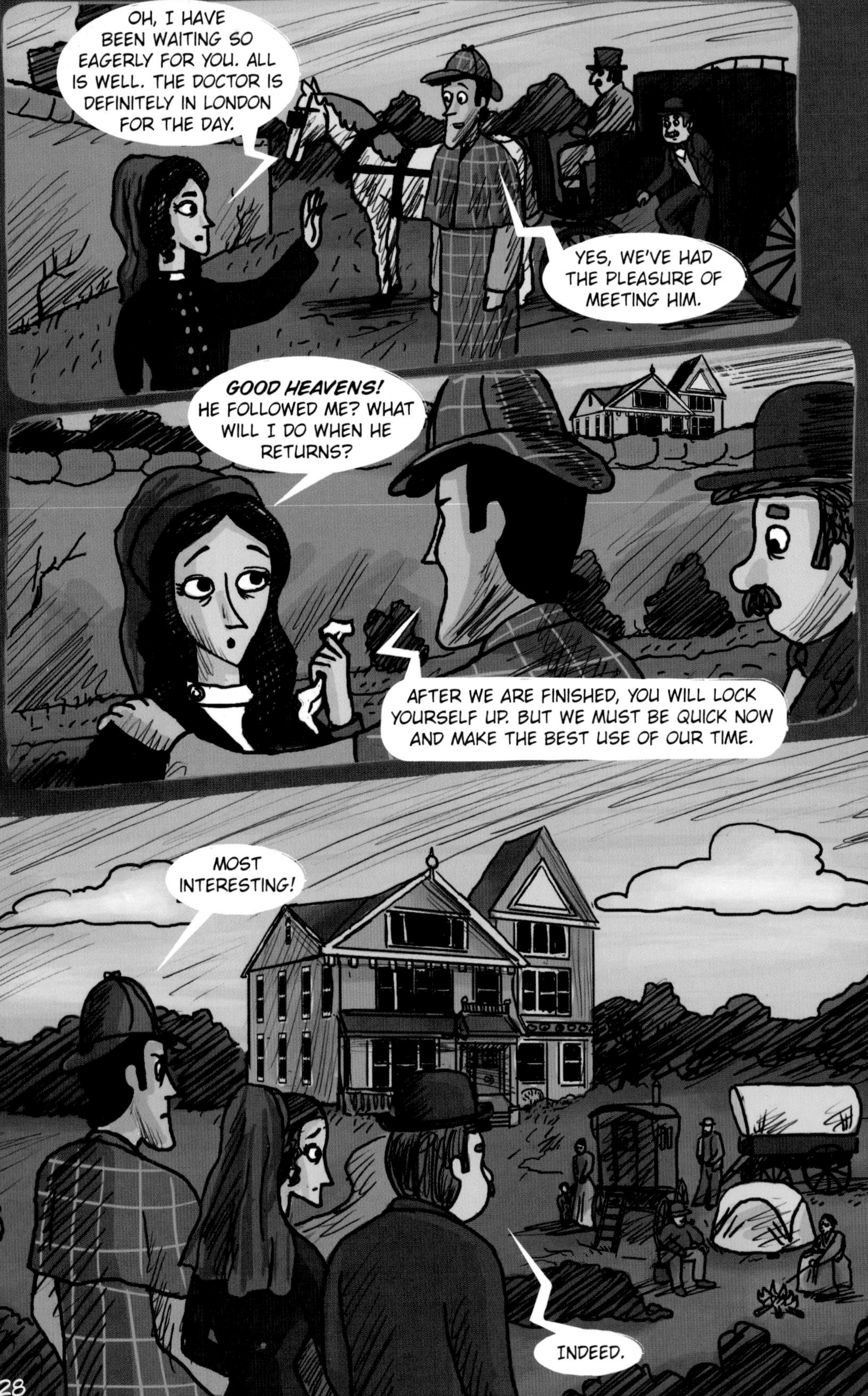
OH, I HAVE BEEN WAITING SO EAGERLY FOR YOU. ALL IS WELL. THE DOCTOR IS DEFINITELY IN LONDON FOR THE DAY.
YES, WE'VE HAD THE PLEASURE OF MEETING HIM.
GOOD HEAVENS! HE FOLLOWED ME? WHAT WILL I DO WHEN HE RETURNS?
AFTER WE ARE FINISHED, YOU WILL LOCK YOURSELF UP. BUT WE MUST BE QUICK NOW AND MAKE THE BEST USE OF OUR TIME.
MOST INTERESTING!
INDEED.

Holmes carefully examined the newer wing—the stone walls, the windows, and the poorly kept lawn. There were no signs of footprints or any kind of disturbance underneath the bedroom windows. He tried forcing the bolted shutters open, but they held tightly. He did notice that a hole had been broken into the outside wall of Helen's bedroom.

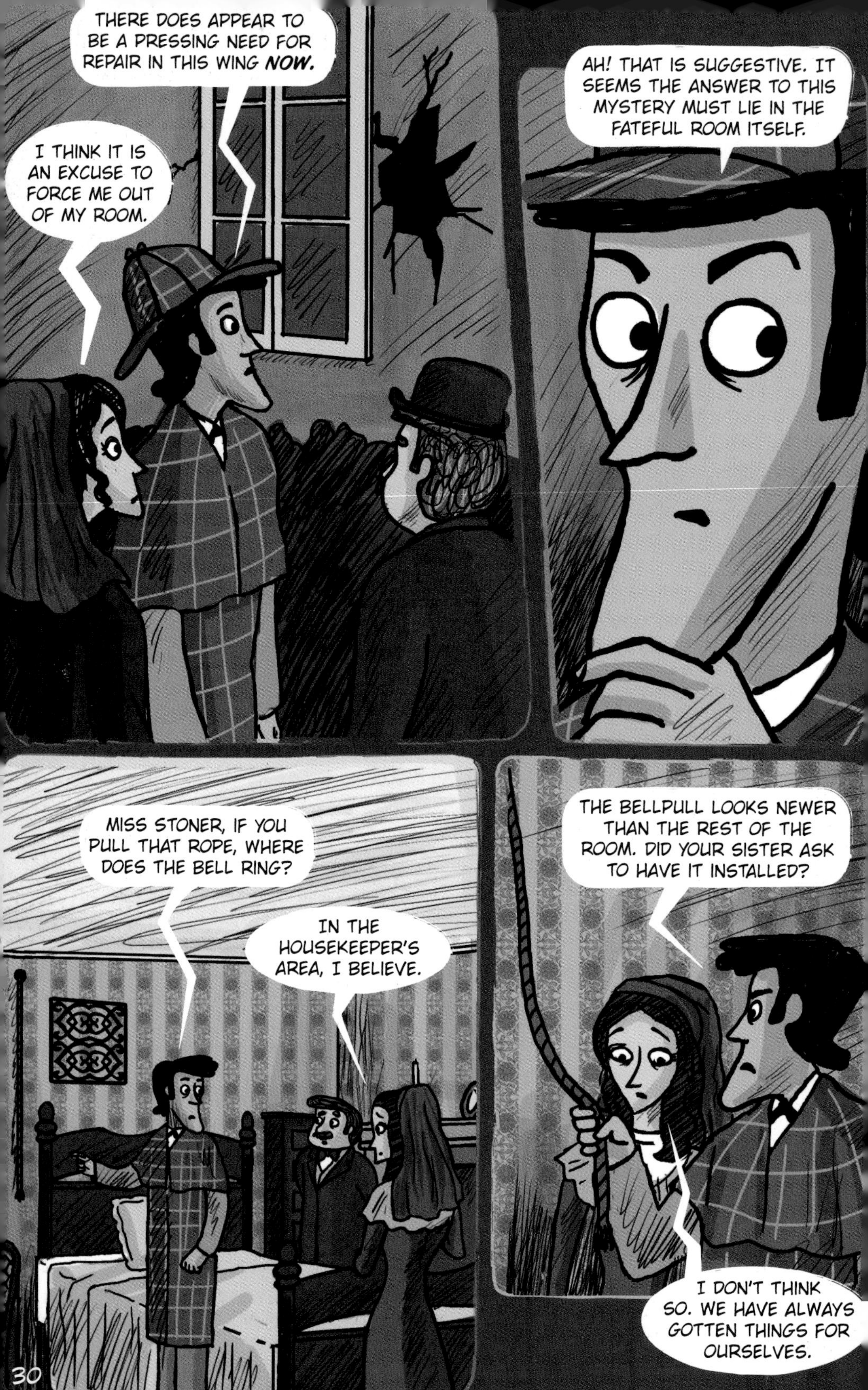
THERE DOES APPEAR TO BE A PRESSING NEED FOR REPAIR IN THIS WING NOW.
I THINK IT IS AN EXCUSE TO FORCE ME OUT OF MY ROOM.
AH! THAT IS SUGGESTIVE. IT SEEMS THE ANSWER TO THIS MYSTERY MUST LIE IN THE FATEFUL ROOM ITSELF.
MISS STONER, IF YOU PULL THAT ROPE, WHERE DOES THE BELL RING?
IN THE HOUSEKEEPER'S AREA, I BELIEVE.
THE BELLPULL LOOKS NEWER THAN THE REST OF THE ROOM. DID YOUR SISTER ASK TO HAVE IT INSTALLED?
I DON'T THINK SO. WE HAVE ALWAYS GOTTEN THINGS FOR OURSELVES.

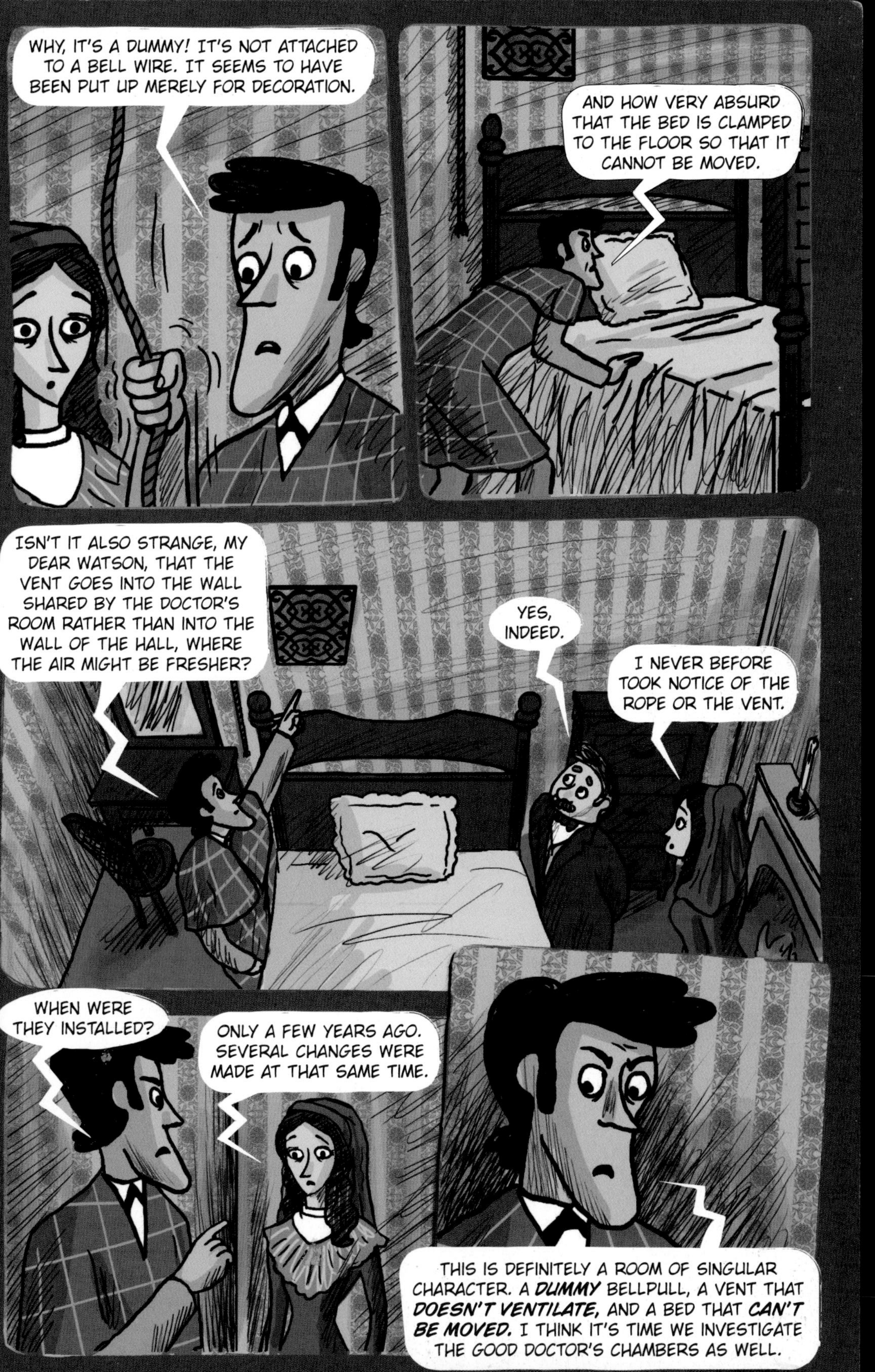
WHY, IT'S A DUMMY! IT'S NOT ATTACHED TO A BELL WIRE. IT SEEMS TO HAVE BEEN PUT UP MERELY FOR DECORATION.
AND HOW VERY ABSURD THAT THE BED IS CLAMPED TO THE FLOOR SO THAT IT CANNOT BE MOVED.
ISN'T IT ALSO STRANGE, MY DEAR WATSON, THAT THE VENT GOES INTO THE WALL SHARED BY THE DOCTOR'S ROOM RATHER THAN INTO THE WALL OF THE HALL, WHERE THE AIR MIGHT BE FRESHER?
YES, INDEED.
I NEVER BEFORE TOOK NOTICE OF THE ROPE OR THE VENT.
WHEN WERE THEY INSTALLED?
ONLY A FEW YEARS AGO. SEVERAL CHANGES WERE MADE AT THAT SAME TIME.
THIS IS DEFINITELY A ROOM OF SINGULAR CHARACTER. A ***DUMMY*** BELLPULL, A VENT THAT ***DOESN'T VENTILATE,*** AND A BED THAT ***CAN'T BE MOVED.*** I THINK IT'S TIME WE INVESTIGATE THE GOOD DOCTOR'S CHAMBERS AS WELL.

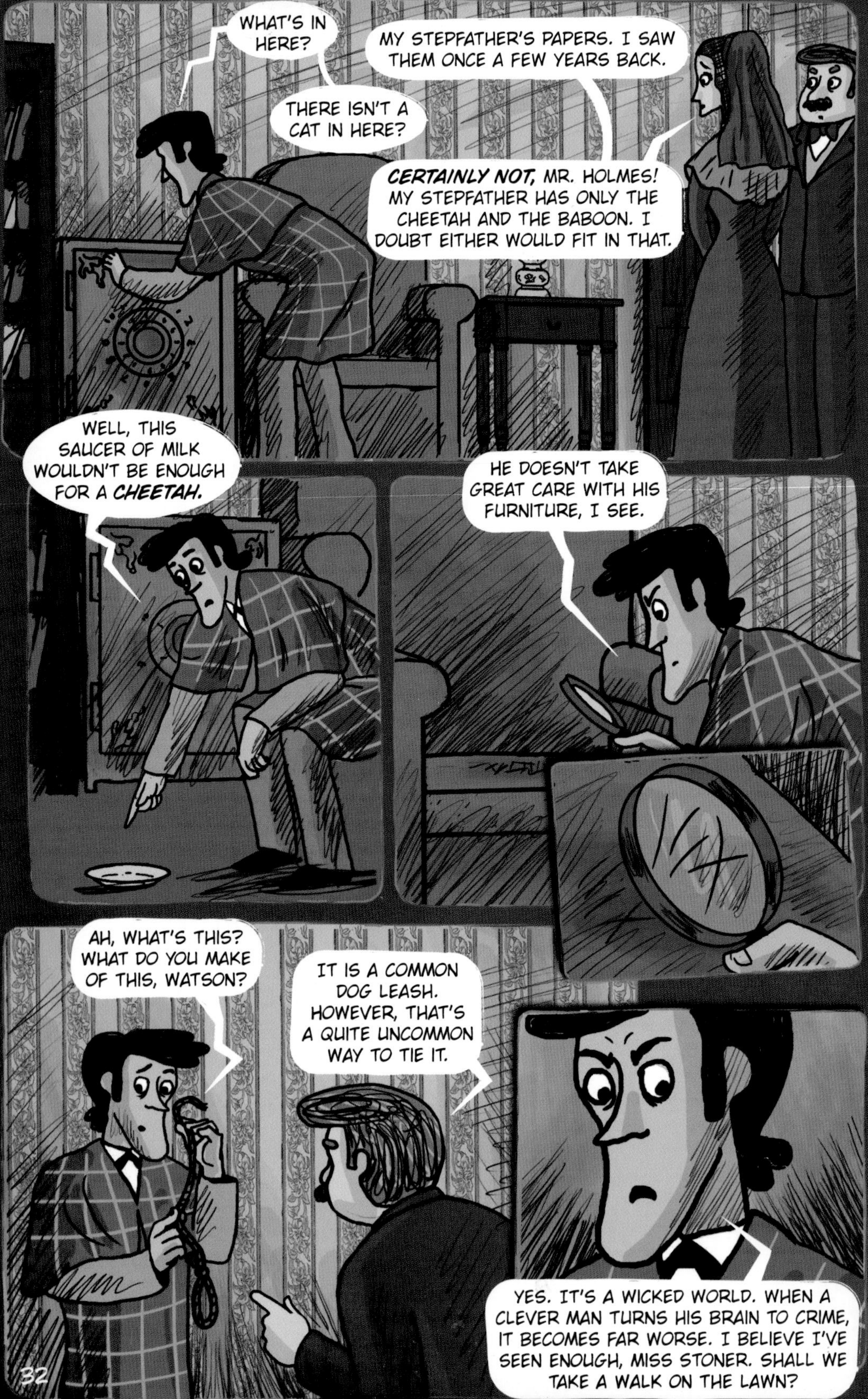

WHAT'S IN HERE?
THERE ISN'T A CAT IN HERE?
MY STEPFATHER'S PAPERS. I SAW THEM ONCE A FEW YEARS BACK.
CERTAINLY NOT, MR. HOLMES! MY STEPFATHER HAS ONLY THE CHEETAH AND THE BABOON. I DOUBT EITHER WOULD FIT IN THAT.
WELL, THIS SAUCER OF MILK WOULDN'T BE ENOUGH FOR A CHEETAH.
HE DOESN'T TAKE GREAT CARE WITH HIS FURNITURE, I SEE.
AH, WHAT'S THIS? WHAT DO YOU MAKE OF THIS, WATSON?
IT IS A COMMON DOG LEASH. HOWEVER, THAT'S A QUITE UNCOMMON WAY TO TIE IT.
YES. IT'S A WICKED WORLD. WHEN A CLEVER MAN TURNS HIS BRAIN TO CRIME, IT BECOMES FAR WORSE. I BELIEVE I'VE SEEN ENOUGH, MISS STONER. SHALL WE TAKE A WALK ON THE LAWN?

I had never seen my friend's face so grim and so dark as it was this day. I was wondering what he knew and what plan he was forming. Miss Stoner, I can well imagine, was placing her trust and her future—in fact, her very life—in the hands of Sherlock Holmes.

Finally, Holmes turned to Miss Stoner. He asked her to leave a note for her stepfather claiming that she had gone to sleep early with a headache and wished not to be disturbed. Then, when she heard her stepfather retire for the evening, she was to open her shutters quietly and set a lamp on the windowsill. Then she was to quietly return to her old room. He told her that he and I would be watching her wing from the Crown Inn across the way. Holmes explained that we would return to the manor and would be spending the night in her sister's room.

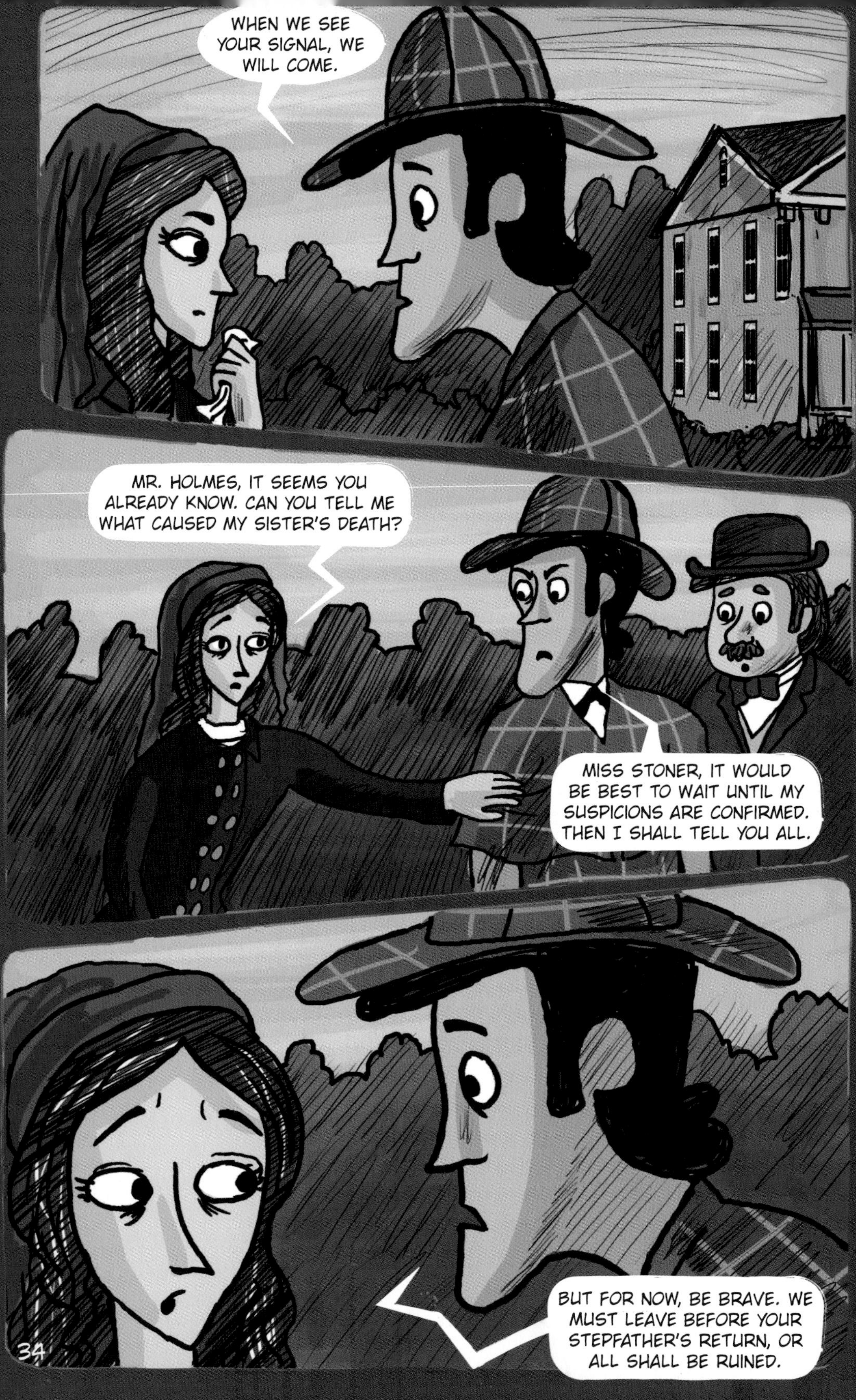
WHEN WE SEE YOUR SIGNAL, WE WILL COME.
MR. HOLMES, IT SEEMS YOU ALREADY KNOW. CAN YOU TELL ME WHAT CAUSED MY SISTER'S DEATH?
MISS STONER, IT WOULD BE BEST TO WAIT UNTIL MY SUSPICIONS ARE CONFIRMED. THEN I SHALL TELL YOU ALL.
BUT FOR NOW, BE BRAVE. WE MUST LEAVE BEFORE YOUR STEPFATHER'S RETURN, OR ALL SHALL BE RUINED.

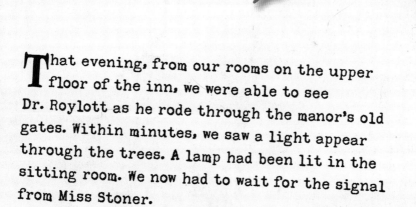

That evening, from our rooms on the upper floor of the inn, we were able to see Dr. Roylott as he rode through the manor's old gates. Within minutes, we saw a light appear through the trees. A lamp had been lit in the sitting room. We now had to wait for the signal from Miss Stoner.

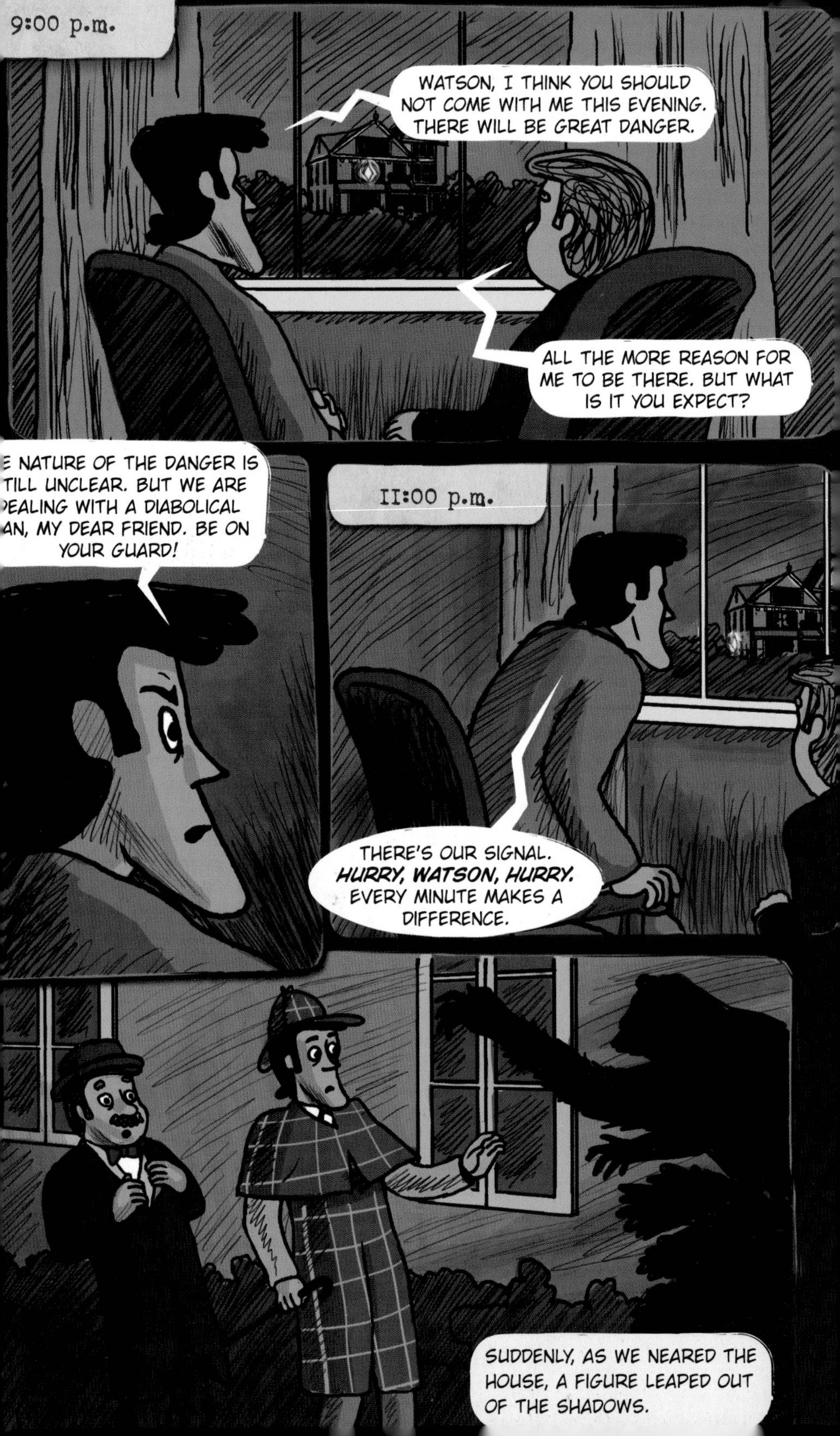
9:00 p.m.
WATSON, I THINK YOU SHOULD NOT COME WITH ME THIS EVENING. THERE WILL BE GREAT DANGER.
ALL THE MORE REASON FOR ME TO BE THERE. BUT WHAT IS IT YOU EXPECT?
E NATURE OF THE DANGER IS TILL UNCLEAR. BUT WE ARE DEALING WITH A DIABOLICAL AN, MY DEAR FRIEND. BE ON YOUR GUARD!
11:00 p.m.
THERE'S OUR SIGNAL. HURRY, WATSON, HURRY. EVERY MINUTE MAKES A DIFFERENCE.
SUDDENLY, AS WE NEARED THE HOUSE, A FIGURE LEAPED OUT OF THE SHADOWS.

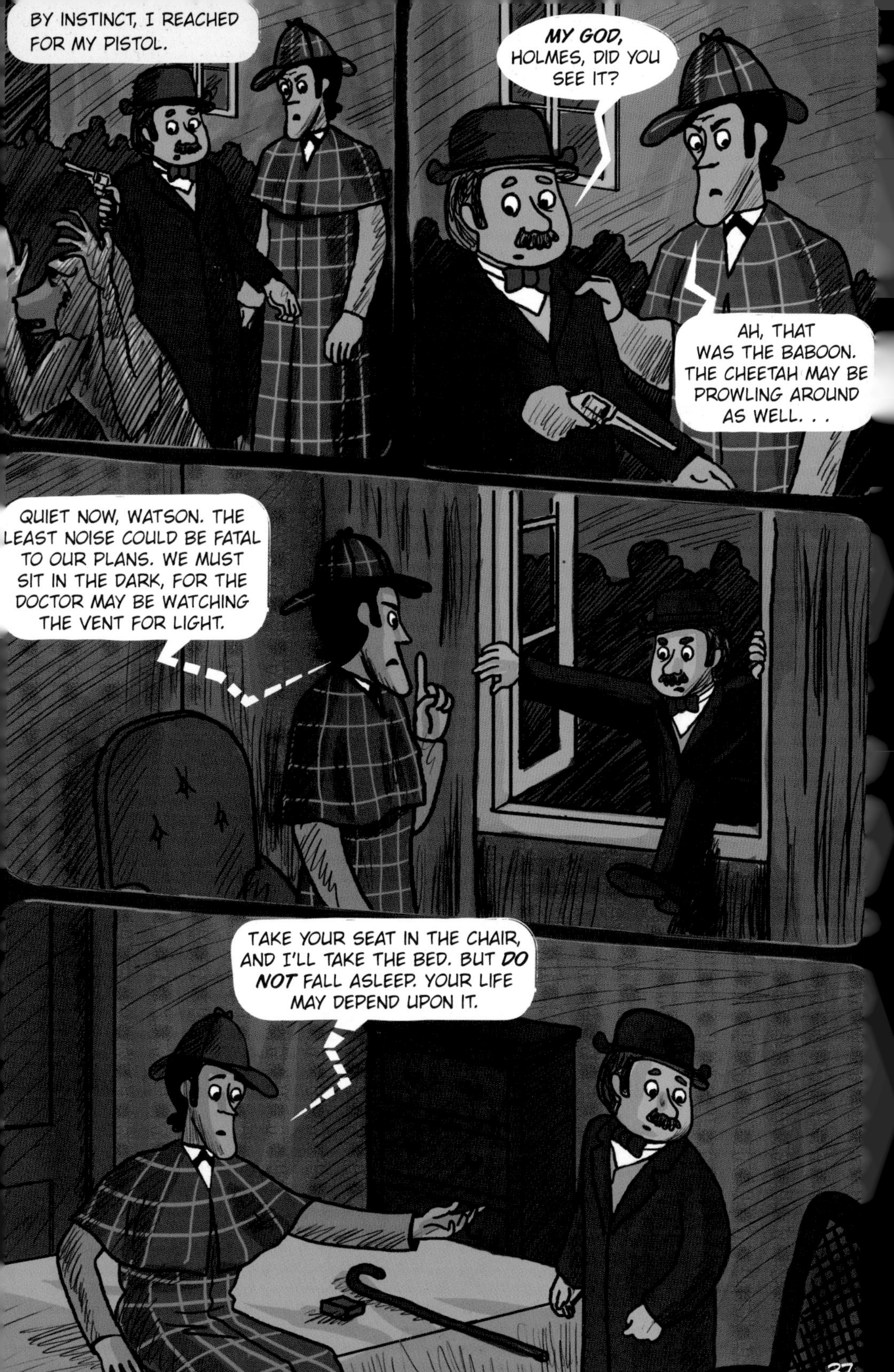
BY INSTINCT, I REACHED FOR MY PISTOL.
MY GOD, HOLMES, DID YOU SEE IT?
AH, THAT WAS THE BABOON. THE CHEETAH MAY BE PROWLING AROUND AS WELL. . .
QUIET NOW, WATSON. THE LEAST NOISE COULD BE FATAL TO OUR PLANS. WE MUST SIT IN THE DARK, FOR THE DOCTOR MAY BE WATCHING THE VENT FOR LIGHT.
TAKE YOUR SEAT IN THE CHAIR, AND I'LL TAKE THE BED. BUT DO NOT FALL ASLEEP. YOUR LIFE MAY DEPEND UPON IT.

How shall I ever forget that dreadful night of waiting? We hardly dared to breathe. Occasionally, we heard the muffled cry of a night bird, and once a long, catlike howl from beneath the window. The cheetah was free indeed.

Every quarter hour, the faraway tones of the village church bell reached us. How long it took for each fifteen minutes to pass! Twelve o'clock eventually sounded—then one, two, and finally three. I struggled to keep my eyes open and my body alert.

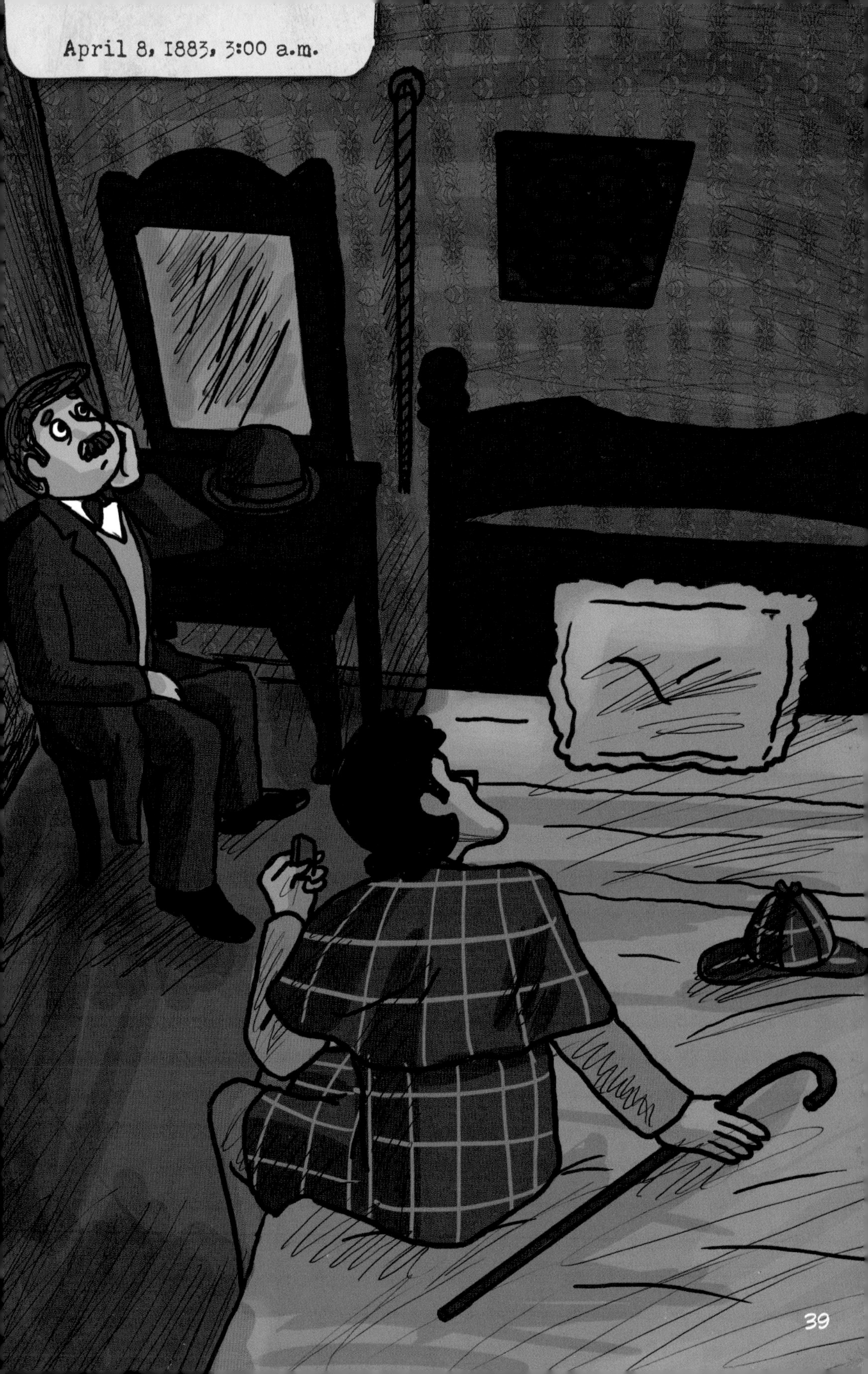
April 8, 1883, 3:00 a.m.

3:30 a.m.

I heard a gentle sound of movement. Then silence. For half an hour we sat, straining to hear something more. At last came a smooth, soothing sound, like hot air escaping from a teakettle. The minute we heard it, Holmes struck a match and lashed savagely at the bellpull with his cane.

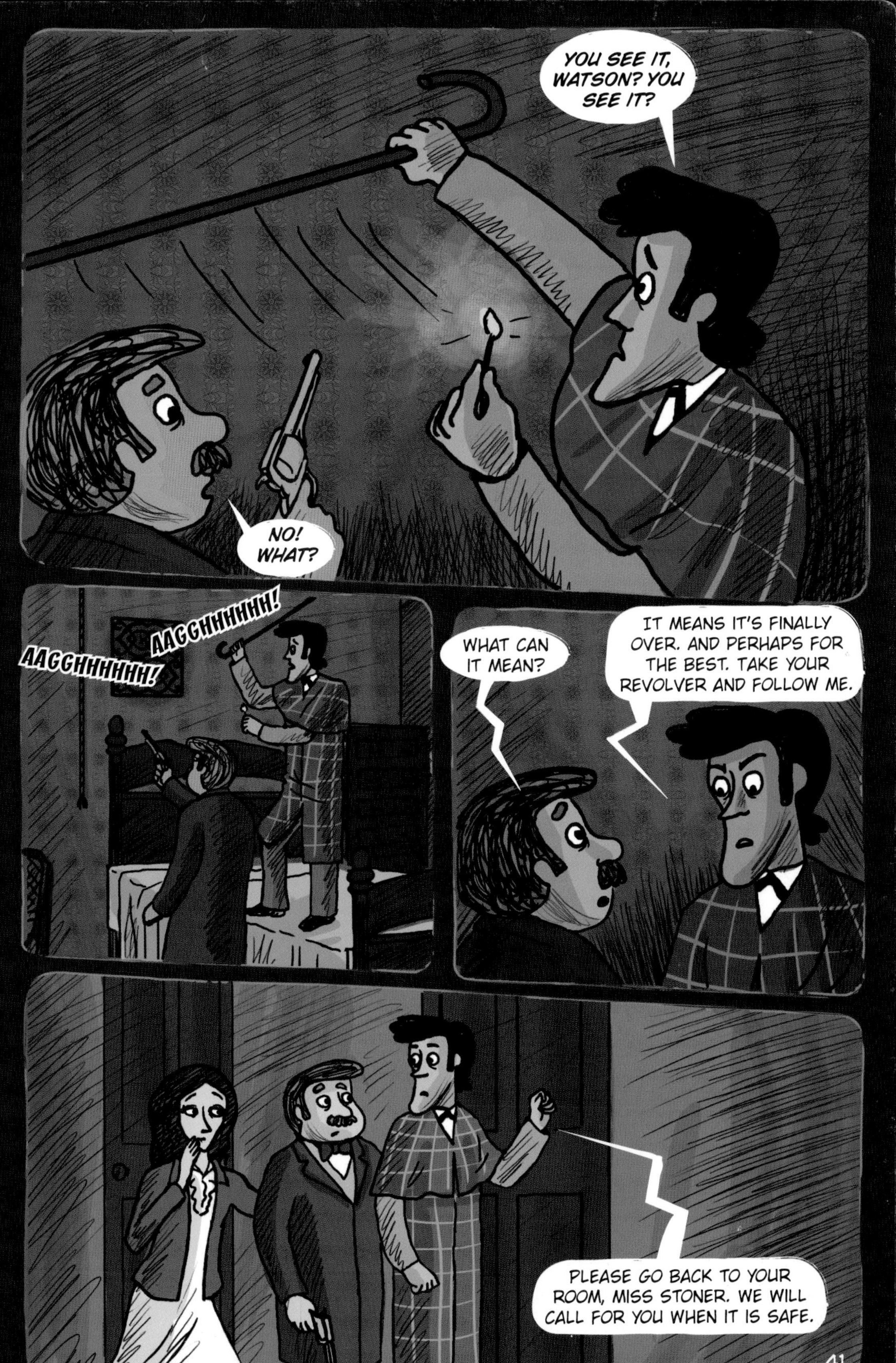

YOU SEE IT, WATSON? YOU SEE IT?
NO! WHAT?
AAGCHHHHHH!
AAGCHHHHHH!
WHAT CAN IT MEAN?
IT MEANS IT'S FINALLY OVER. AND PERHAPS FOR THE BEST. TAKE YOUR REVOLVER AND FOLLOW ME.
PLEASE GO BACK TO YOUR ROOM, MISS STONER. WE WILL CALL FOR YOU WHEN IT IS SAFE.

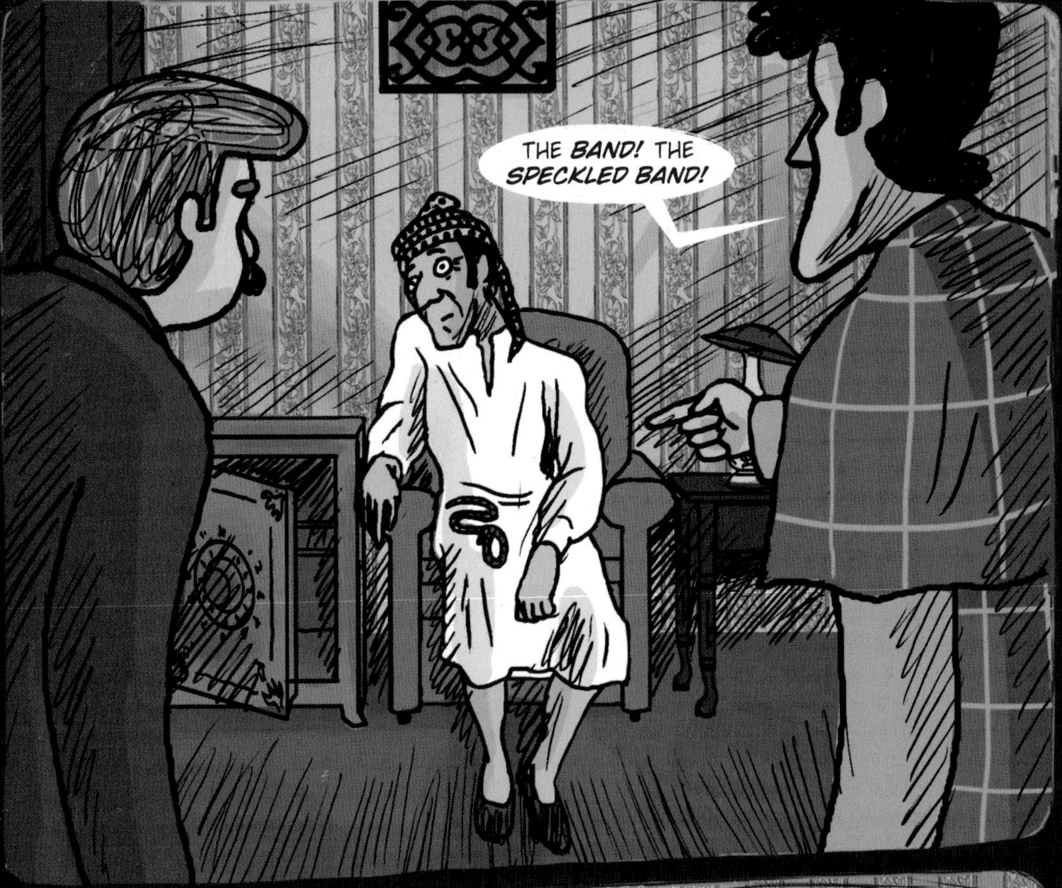
THE *BAND!* THE *SPECKLED BAND!*

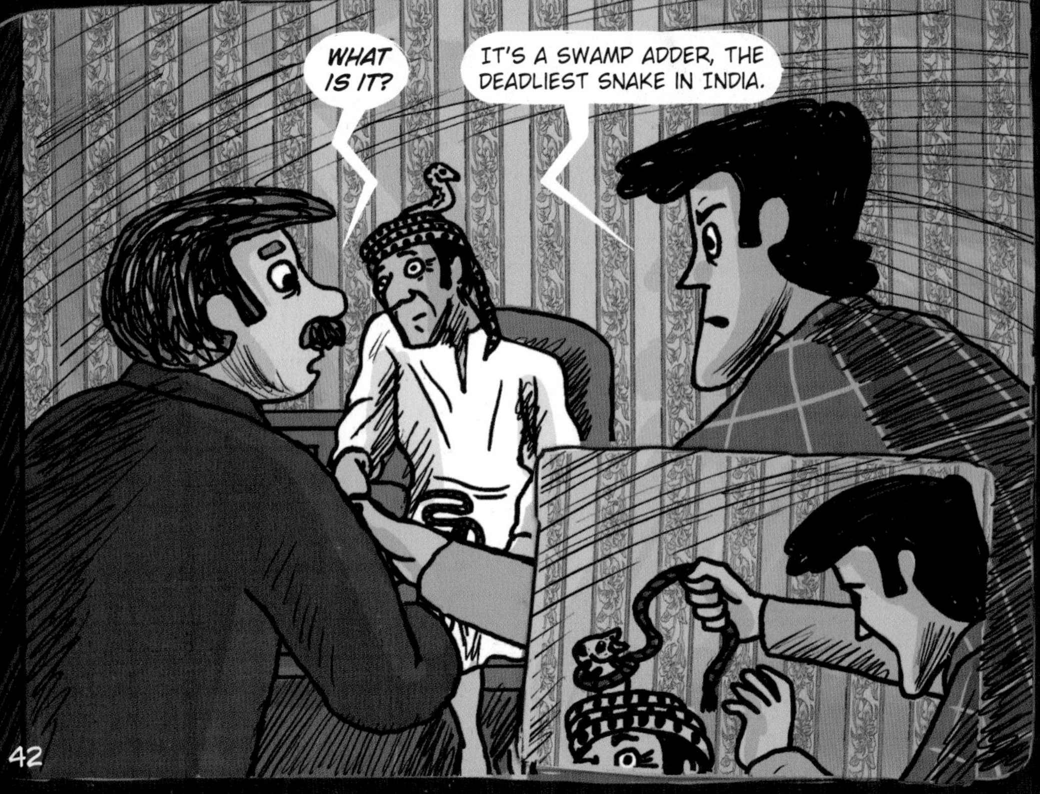
WHAT IS IT?
IT'S A SWAMP ADDER, THE DEADLIEST SNAKE IN INDIA.

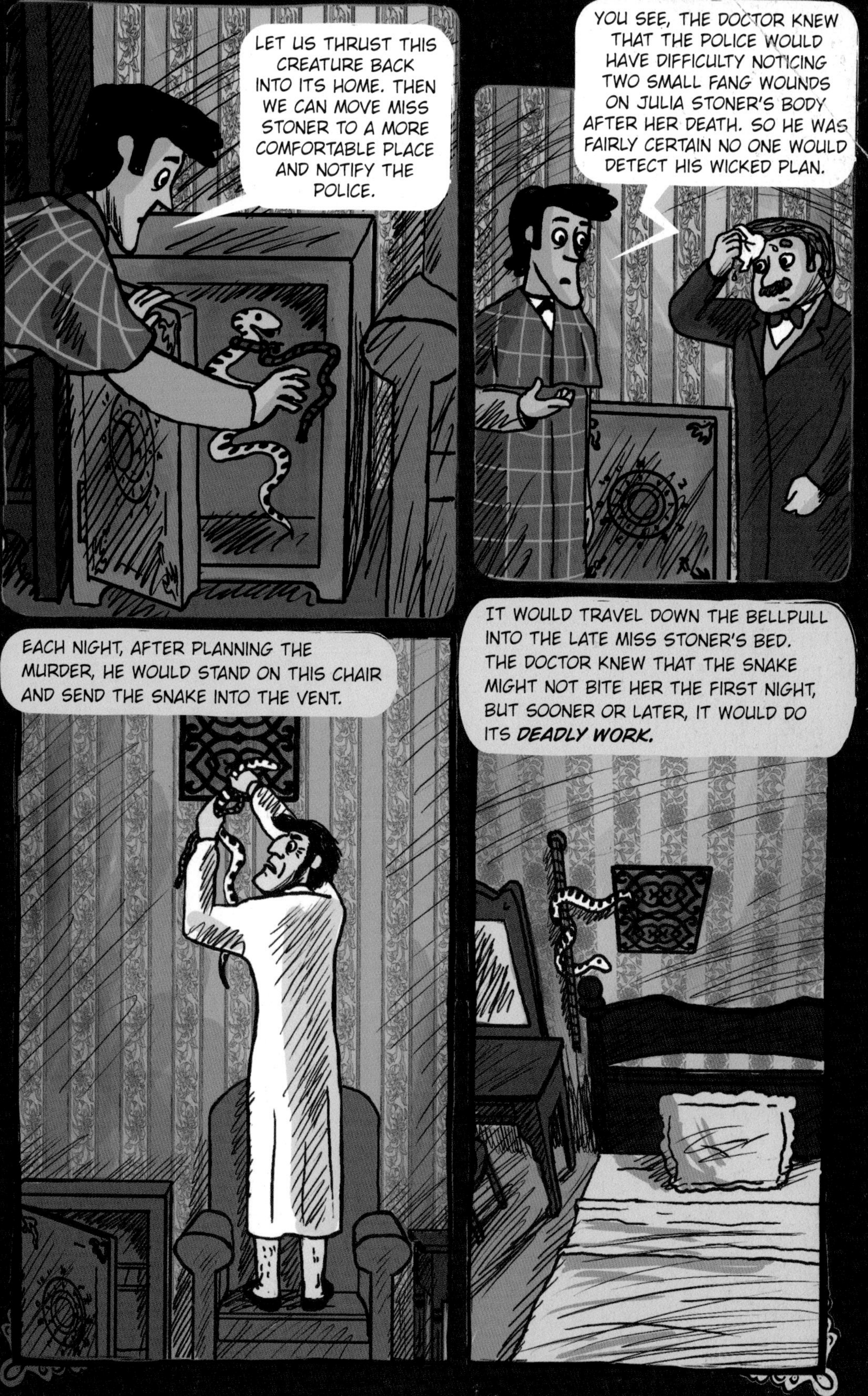
LET US THRUST THIS CREATURE BACK INTO ITS HOME. THEN WE CAN MOVE MISS STONER TO A MORE COMFORTABLE PLACE AND NOTIFY THE POLICE.
YOU SEE, THE DOCTOR KNEW THAT THE POLICE WOULD HAVE DIFFICULTY NOTICING TWO SMALL FANG WOUNDS ON JULIA STONER'S BODY AFTER HER DEATH. SO HE WAS FAIRLY CERTAIN NO ONE WOULD DETECT HIS WICKED PLAN.
EACH NIGHT, AFTER PLANNING THE MURDER, HE WOULD STAND ON THIS CHAIR AND SEND THE SNAKE INTO THE VENT.
IT WOULD TRAVEL DOWN THE BELLPULL INTO THE LATE MISS STONER'S BED. THE DOCTOR KNEW THAT THE SNAKE MIGHT NOT BITE HER THE FIRST NIGHT, BUT SOONER OR LATER, IT WOULD DO ITS ***DEADLY WORK.***

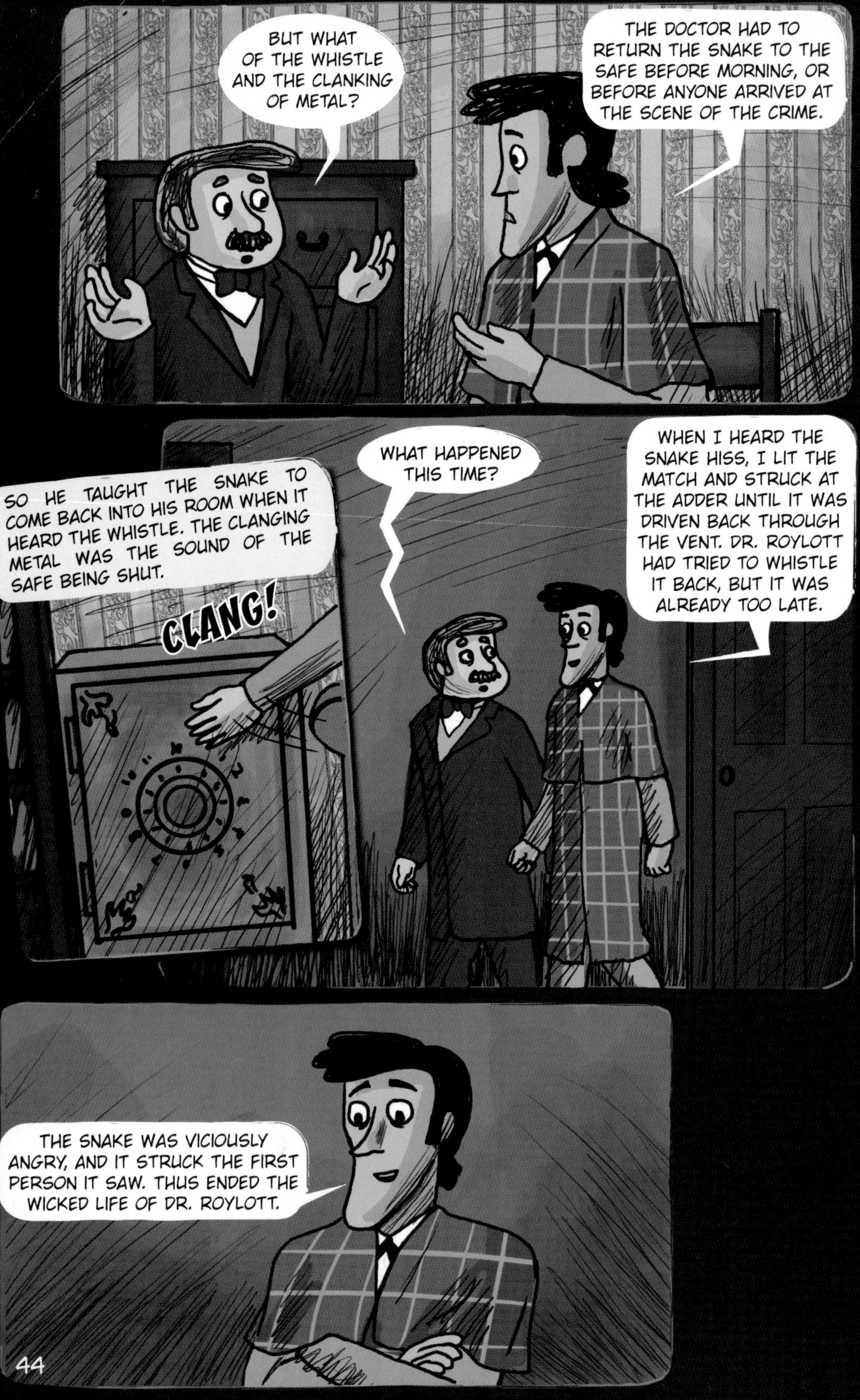
BUT WHAT OF THE WHISTLE AND THE CLANKING OF METAL?
THE DOCTOR HAD TO RETURN THE SNAKE TO THE SAFE BEFORE MORNING, OR BEFORE ANYONE ARRIVED AT THE SCENE OF THE CRIME.
SO HE TAUGHT THE SNAKE TO COME BACK INTO HIS ROOM WHEN IT HEARD THE WHISTLE. THE CLANGING METAL WAS THE SOUND OF THE SAFE BEING SHUT.
CLANG!
WHAT HAPPENED THIS TIME?
WHEN I HEARD THE SNAKE HISS, I LIT THE MATCH AND STRUCK AT THE ADDER UNTIL IT WAS DRIVEN BACK THROUGH THE VENT. DR. ROYLOTT HAD TRIED TO WHISTLE IT BACK, BUT IT WAS ALREADY TOO LATE.
THE SNAKE WAS VICIOUSLY ANGRY, AND IT STRUCK THE FIRST PERSON IT SAW. THUS ENDED THE WICKED LIFE OF DR. ROYLOTT.

Such are the true facts of the death of Dr. Grimesby Roylott. Holmes and I delivered Miss Stoner to her aunt's home at Harrow, and the young woman eventually married Percy Armitage. The police made an official investigation of the doctor's death. Their report concluded that Dr. Roylott met his fate while unwisely playing with a dangerous pet.

From the Desk of
John H. Watson, M.D.

The Adventure of the Speckled Band: How Did Holmes Solve It?

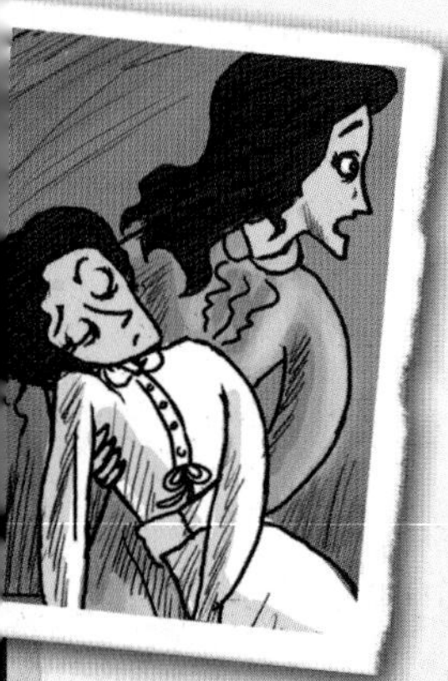

Why did Holmes suspect murder?

It seemed unlikely that a healthy young woman would die of nervous shock, so Holmes suspected foul play immediately. Dr. Roylott was Holmes's first suspect. The man had a violent temper. He had already killed one person. When Holmes read the mother's will, he found that the doctor had money to gain by killing one or both of the sisters.

What did Holmes conclude from examining Julia's room?

From the beginning, Holmes thought there must be a secret opening to Julia's room. She had smelled the doctor's cigars from her room, for example. This led Holmes to discover the vent.

When Holmes discovered that the bellpull was a fake, he knew he was on to something. And the rope and the vent had been installed at the same time. Therefore, it was likely that they had been installed for the same purpose! Holmes also noted that the bed was clamped to the floor. Because of this, anyone sleeping in the bedroom had to sleep under the fake bellpull.

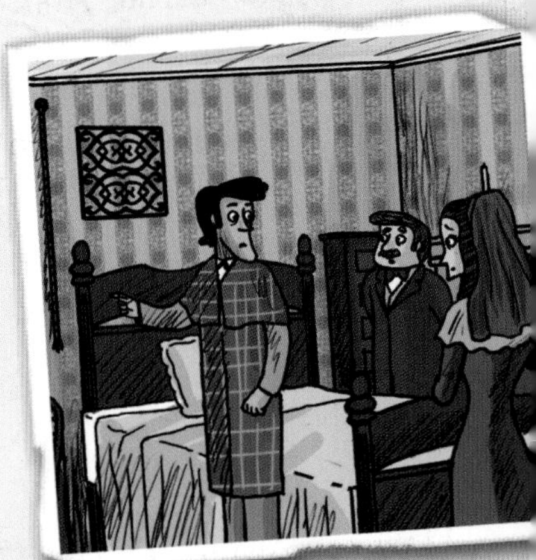

How did Holmes know that a swamp adder had killed Julia?

Holmes figured out that the vent, the bellpull, and the bed were a bridge from Dr. Roylott to the murder victim. The doctor couldn't go through the vent, but a trained pet could. Suddenly, the low whistle fit into the puzzle. It was the doctor's signal to his pet.

Holmes's final clues were found in the doctor's room. The milk in the dish confirmed that an animal was being fed. The scratched chair showed that the doctor probably stood on his chair to put his pet into the vent. One question remained: What animal could fit through the vent? Holmes had his answer when he saw the loop at the end of the leash. Many people use small nooses such as this to handle snakes.

Further Reading and Websites

MacMillan, Dianne M. *Cheetahs*. Minneapolis: Lerner Publications Company, 2009.

Montgomery, Sy, and Nic Bishop. *The Snake Scientist*. Boston: Houghton Mifflin, 2001.

PBS History Detectives
http://pbskids.org/historydetectives

Sherlock Holmes Museum
http://www.sherlock-holmes.co.uk

Singer, Marilyn. *Venom*. Minneapolis: Millbrook Press, 2007.

Stewart, Melissa. *Baboons*. Minneapolis: Lerner Publications Company, 2007.

Souza, D. M. *Packed with Poison: Deadly Animal Defenses*. Minneapolis: Millbrook Press, 2006.

Time for Kids Around the World: India
http://www.timeforkids.com/TFK/specials/goplaces/0,12405,214513,00.html

221 Baker Street
http://221bakerstreet.org

White, Nancy. *Death Adders: Super Deadly!* New York: Bearport Publishing Company, 2009.

About the Author

Sir Arthur Conan Doyle was born on May 22, 1859. He became a doctor in 1882. When this career did not prove successful, Doyle started writing stories. In addition to the popular Sherlock Holmes short stories and novels, Doyle also wrote historical novels, romances, and plays.

About the Adapters

Murray Shaw's lifelong passion for Sherlock Holmes began when he was a child. He was the author of the Match Wits with Sherlock Holmes series published in the 1990s. For decades, he was a popular speaker in public schools and libraries on the adventures of Holmes and Watson.

M. J. Cosson is the author of more than fifty books, both fiction and nonfiction, for children and young adults. She has long been a fan of mysteries and especially of the great detective, Sherlock Holmes. In fact, she has participated in the production of several Sherlock Holmes plays. A native of Iowa, Cosson lives in the Texas Hill Country with her husband, dogs, and cat.

About the Illustrator

French artist Sophie Rohrbach began her career after graduating in display design at the Chambre des Commerce. She went on to design displays in many top department stores including Galeries Lafayette. She also studied illustration at Emile Cohl school in Lyon, France, where she now lives with her daughter. Rohrbach has illustrated many children's books. She is passionate about the colors and patterns that she uses in her illustrations.